Thirteen tales of
genteel magics,
deathly pets, mysterious
contraptions, and one ever
so heroic noveltrix, to ease the
melancholy of the Great Pause.
Come within. Set down your cares.
You may be obliged for a fortnight.

We have tea.

Curiosities #7 Quarantine 2020

Cover art by Tracy Whiteside
Illustrative Collages by Martini Discovolante

ISBN-13:978-1-948396-11-0 (Print on Demand)

Messrs. Frost & McCurdy are pleased to present

Table of Contents

Natasha C. Calder

The Death Trade

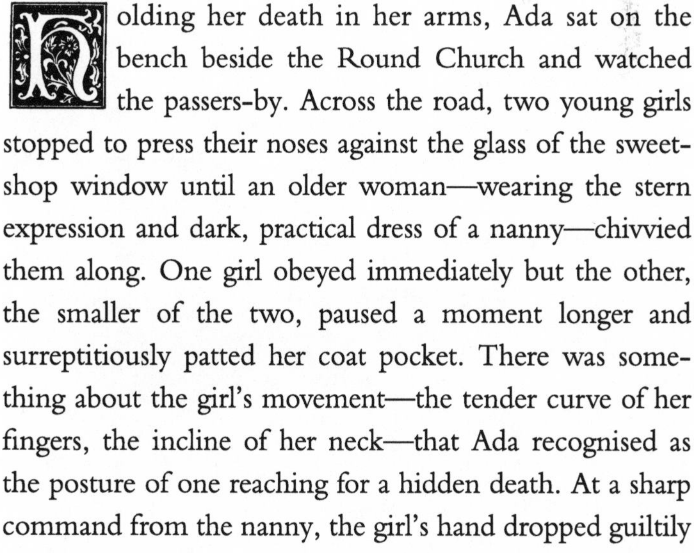

Holding her death in her arms, Ada sat on the bench beside the Round Church and watched the passers-by. Across the road, two young girls stopped to press their noses against the glass of the sweet-shop window until an older woman—wearing the stern expression and dark, practical dress of a nanny—chivvied them along. One girl obeyed immediately but the other, the smaller of the two, paused a moment longer and surreptitiously patted her coat pocket. There was something about the girl's movement—the tender curve of her fingers, the incline of her neck—that Ada recognised as the posture of one reaching for a hidden death. At a sharp command from the nanny, the girl's hand dropped guiltily from her pocket to her side. She hitched her skirts and hurried to catch up, vanishing down St John's Street with a flash of white muslin.

Ada remembered what her own death had been like at that age; a helpless thing with fur like lilac smoke and so small that she could carry it in the palm of one hand. By the time of her thirteenth birthday, of course, her death had grown too large to be easily concealed in a coat pocket. That was when she'd been given her first proper dress, with wide sleeves that fell down past the knuckles such that she could carry her death in the crook of her arm or curled around her wrist and it would be kept safely out of sight.

Although Ada was nearly twenty now, her death had grown little in the intervening years. The lilac had darkened to a deep violet that was sometimes rippled through with indigo and its form had started to become a little clearer, paws and muzzle materialising out of the soft haze of shadow. But it was still no longer than her forearm and still spent most of its time contentedly asleep. At least she thought it was asleep. Given that it had yet to develop eyes, it was near impossible to tell. She should have been glad—a stunted death was a sure sign of a long, healthy life—and yet her sentiments tended more towards dissatisfaction. Much as she might wish it were otherwise, she knew hers was the death of one who had seen little of life.

A gentleman wearing a scholar's gown trimmed in Magdalene colours came down the pavement on the far side of the wall that bordered the church yard. He was not the man she was waiting for—that much was evident from the sleekness of the death draped about his neck—and he sneered disdainfully at Ada as he passed. She resisted the urge to sneer back. Of all the scholars she had encountered, it was only the men of Magdalene who made a point of being affronted by the sight of a woman's death. Most colleges nurtured a more daring outlook—it was even said the lady scholars of Corpus Christi and King's wore their deaths like stoles inside the college grounds and no one so much as raised an eyebrow—but Magdalene remained staunch in its support of the belief commonly held by wider society: that no civilised woman should bare her death.

Usually, Ada only dared walk about with her death on show when she was wearing one of Charlie's suits. She would braid her auburn hair neatly on top of her head, conceal it beneath a flat cap and cut through the market square with her death in plain view on her shoulder, her heart beating in her throat, her eyes wild with the exquisite fear of being caught. Today, however, she was wearing an old calico dress of simple design, one that had already been threadbare and faded when it was first given her. Since then, she'd worn it so often to cart bootleg gin to Charlie's customers in Grantchester that the hem was stained with mud from the path that ran through the meadows. So long as she took care to moderate her posture and expression, the dress's ragged appearance was enough to transform her into a lowly beggar. It was her most serviceable disguise for trading her death.

There had, of course, been no need for such a disguise in the very first trade. It had happened nearly a year ago, when the son of one of Charlie's London associates, due to sit the entrance examinations for King's, came to stay with them in Romsey Road. Ada had never met the boy's father—one Mr McLeever—but Charlie's associates were all brutes of one sort or another. So it was something of a surprise when the boy proved to be a bright young thing, expensively educated and with a gentle manner that reminded Ada of the dull, soft-spoken aristocratic boys she had grown up with. All the same, the boy inspired a sort of instinctive affection in her that was in no small part related to the fact he possessed a death already as large as Charlie's own.

Like so many men, Charlie had returned from France with a death like an attack dog, all fury and wicked teeth. But the McLeever boy was too young to have fought, too young for the death he carried. Although a death could be quickened or stunted for any number of reasons, in most minds a young face with a death so grotesque meant only one thing: the deprivation of poverty. No matter how bright the boy was or how adeptly he answered the questions put to him, not one of the colleges would touch him—not even King's—not with a death like his.

For Ada—who was, by then, well accustomed to walking disguised—the solution came readily. The boy merely needed to carry her death in place of his own to the exams and the college dons would be none the wiser. She'd put the idea to Charlie and he flatly forbade it. Ada, determined that she be allowed to shoulder her own risks, had been ready for his refusal, quietly explaining that she had no intention of allowing another man to touch her death. The boy would carry it in a set of panniers, which was all the fashion amongst the younger scholars, invariably keen cyclists who enjoyed the ease of being able to sling a pair of saddle bags over a back wheel at a moment's notice. Ada rather thought it was also preferred as a means of demonstrating vigour, for only a healthy death could fit inside a set of panniers and only a healthy death, having not yet developed the strength and agency to move unaided, needed to be carried. Whether or not this was the case, the panniers helped make the plan more palatable and, eventually, she persuaded Charlie to give his permission.

On the day of the exams, the boy locked his death in his room. Ada cupped her own death in her hands and placed it securely into a set of purpose-bought panniers, which the boy took from her with careful reverence. Thinking little of what would happen next beyond her own excitement at the daring of it, she sent him off with a wave and a packet of sandwiches wrapped in paper. And then, in the long hours that followed, Ada discovered the sweet agony of being parted from her death.

Despite its absence, she continued to feel its ghostly weight in the crook of her arm. She kept reaching into her sleeve to stroke its fur and being surprised every time her fingers closed on thin air. Not being able to see or touch her death agitated her to the point where she found herself pacing the kitchen floor, compulsively worrying the collar of her dress between finger and thumb. The intensity of it was surpassed only by the relief that flooded her when the boy finally returned, a relief so overwhelming that she hadn't been able to resist scooping up her death and burying her face in its smoky fur. Apparently not having suffered the same agitation, the boy stared. Ada didn't care. *Yes,* she thought, *this is what it means to live; to suffer and to overcome, to know and endure the pain of mortal existence.* The sensation was intoxicating, nearly enough to make up for the long, lifeless years she'd spent trapped in the decorous confines of her father's home, and before long the need to feel it anew would come to consume her.

In that moment, though, she was simply happy. What's more, the ploy worked; the boy was offered a place. It caused quite a stir when he turned up at the start of term with his true death in tow but, by that point, the dons could hardly rescind their offer. Mr McLeever sent flowers and even Charlie offered her a word or two of praise. And then, a few weeks later, he came up with a new plan.

"I've been thinking about what you did for the McLeever boy," he said one evening as he unlaced his boots.

"Oh?"

"Strikes me there are many more who'd benefit from the loan of a young, healthy death. Some of them would pay over the odds for it, too."

Ada sat perfectly still on the edge of the bed, watching as Charlie unfastened the buttons that ran down the front of his shirt, his silver signet ring glinting in the light. "I thought you didn't like me making the trade," she said carefully.

His death reared its head from where it lay coiled at his feet. Charlie reached a calming hand to it, his fingertips brushing dark fur. Then he turned his pale eyes onto Ada. "Since when did you care what I like?"

That had been the end of the discussion. In the following days, weeks and months, Ada had loaned out her death numerous times—mostly to wealthy, older gentlemen of fractious disposition. There had been businessmen needing to prove their vitality to their investors, philanderers eager to demonstrate their virility to their mistresses, and several of Charlie's associates who sought to ease their applications to various gentlemen's clubs by concealing the evidence of their more humble origins. Their deaths were invariably advanced and grim, such that the men themselves seemed only too pleased to get away from them, and Ada quickly grew accustomed to shepherding them around as if they were her own, which in turn afforded new delight. People took one look at her and saw tragedy; a young, pretty woman with a terrible death. And begging on the pavement in her ragged dress, no one ever recognised her. Once the mayor's wife had thrown her tuppence without so much as a second glance, even though the two women had spoken at length when Charlie had taken Ada to the Newmarket Races. The efficacy of the deception was every bit as thrilling as it was when she donned one of Charlie's suits.

Ada spent many of the fallow hours between trades dreaming of the next. Her customers, she noticed, did not exhibit the same agitation upon leaving their deaths behind and only returned to them with reluctance. Accordingly, she was always careful to hide how she longed for the fierce pain and joy of being separated from and reunited with her death. No one but she knew exactly how much she'd come to rely on that rush of fear and relief. And if Charlie *did* notice something was amiss, he turned a blind eye. The trades made good money; the men paid Charlie upwards of a pound an hour, of which he kept half and gave the rest to Ada. It was a steady income, one that Ada supplemented with the money she made begging. Charlie didn't know about that—he'd have stopped her if he had—and Ada made sure he didn't find out. The opportunity to make extra was too good to miss. She told herself it was an escape fund, like the one she'd squirreled away when preparing to flee her father's house, and that she knew better than to trust a man like Charlie Bowman with her future. In truth she was simply hooked. Every coin offered as comfort seemed to weight the scales in her favour, to bring into closer alignment the actuality of her appearance with her vision of herself. Not the bored daughter of a minor aristocrat, but a real woman, occupying a physical space in the world and standing to her share of suffering along with the rest. The coins were proof, and she kept them in a box under a loose floorboard in the bedroom, along with the unopened letters from her mother.

Now, as she sat waiting for her next customer, Ada wondered how much longer she could keep trading her death. As much as she might wish it would grow into a snarling, yellow-eyed beast like Charlie's, she knew that its youth and health were, for now, all that made her useful. But perhaps if she became pregnant...She'd seen the young women walking up and down Romsey Road, their bellies swollen and their deaths too large to conceal, loping along behind them on all fours with pelts that gleamed blood red in the sun. Charlie once said that they reminded him of how the men's deaths had grown to look in the trenches. Even if the women did survive giving birth, their deaths would never recover to what they once had been. The idea filled Ada with a heady mix of desire and dread.

"Mrs Bowman?"

Starting at the sound of Charlie's last name pronounced by an unfamiliar voice, Ada looked up to see an elderly gentleman standing before her. His hair was grey and there were dark rings under his eyes. He looked as thin and tired as his death was powerful and alert. This had to be the man. "Call me Ada," she said.

He bowed his head, offered his own name in return and then pointed at the space on the bench beside her. "May I?"

"Please."

The man sat with obvious relief and Ada noticed his breath was strained and arduous. She was used to trading with men who—no matter how grim the deaths they bore—spoke with the self-assured confidence of those accustomed to getting their own way. But this man's tone was gentle and courteous.

"Forgive me," he said. "I am not well. I do not think I have much time left."

Ada believed him. His death had the same watchful stillness that her grandmother's had adopted in her last days and Ada regarded it with an intense curiosity. She'd been barred from the room when her grandmother died, her father claiming that it was not fit or safe for one with a young, impressionable death. Although she'd heard stories of how a death transformed in its final moments—the sudden engorgement, the savagery—she longed to witness it for herself. In just a few days, she thought, this man would die and see that alteration first hand. Why, he barely looked fit enough to carry the panniers and was clearly in no position to go ahead with the trade, which was a shame. With a death like his at her side, she could make a killing.

Thinking it best to cut her losses, she adopted a bright manner and sought to send him on his way, offering to release him from their agreement and saying she was sure Charlie would return his money when she explained the circumstances.

The man shook his head. "I'm due to meet my nephew within the hour. He's not seen me in many years and knows nothing of my illness. I don't want him to worry. Nor do I wish him to take word to his mother—my sister—and cause *her* to worry. Not before it's time."

Ada said nothing to this. The man might be able to hide his death but he couldn't hide the gaunt pallor of his face or the incessant tremor of his hands. Apparently thinking along similar lines, he glanced down at Ada's death in her lap and emitted a soft, wheezing laugh. "Though I'm not sure my nephew will believe I have *quite* such a fine death as yours."

Unbidden, an image sprang into Ada's mind of herself hunched on the pavement, the terrible creature stretched out beside her, and her heart swelled with longing. It really was too good an opportunity to miss. Finally, she relented. "The panniers hide most of it," she explained, indicating the leather bags slung over the back of the bench. "Your nephew will never notice."

He gave a weak smile. "I see you've thought of everything. And I simply leave Yorick here with you?"

Ada was about to ask what he meant and then stopped herself, suddenly certain of his meaning. The man was referring to his death. He had *named* it, as though it were nothing more than a child or a pet. Ada had never heard of such a thing. A death was a part of you, as much as the heart in your chest or the brain in your skull. Such things were beyond names.

Seeing her confusion, the man leant in a little closer. "I know it isn't usual. It started as a foolish joke. *Hamlet,* you know. But then the name stuck. The more I called him Yorick, the more he seemed to *be* a Yorick. The more he seemed to be...well...a *he.*"

"I see," lied Ada. She looked from the man to his grey death and then to her own, curled sleepily in her lap. It was hers and she felt a deep pang of affection for it, but she could no more name it than she could her left elbow. For the man to have named his death... it suggested a fondness that was at odds with his manner, for whenever his eyes fell on the creature his expression became drawn and fearful. She didn't see what was so funny about the name, either. Maybe you had to know *Hamlet* to get the joke. Still, if it brought him some kind of comfort, then she wasn't going to argue. "Well, yes, sir. You just leave your... Yorick with me. I'll take care of it...*him*...and meet you here in...two hours, I think Charlie said?"

"Yes," said the man. "Two hours should be more than sufficient. We shall be dining in the University Arms, should you need to find me before then."

With a nod, Ada picked up her death and tucked it into the nearest pannier. Then she helped the man to his feet and placed the panniers over his shoulder. He stooped a little under the weight and then smiled, the skin around his eyes creasing. "Thank you," he said. "You've been ever so kind."

He set off down the road in the direction of Parker's

Piece, the vast common that bordered the old town centre. Ada watched until he was out of sight, welcoming the familiar tightening grip around her heart as her death was taken further and further away. Then she looked back at the man's death, sitting obediently where it had been left. Yorick. At least its ridiculous name didn't diminish the severity of its appearance.

Settling herself on the pavement with her back to the wall and the man's death beside her, Ada allowed the anguish of separation to warp her expression into something forlorn and desolate. A passing Magdalene scholar —he could have been the very twin of the man who'd sneered at her not twenty minutes before—took one look at the death and tossed a coin into her lap, his brow sympathetically furrowed. It occurred to Ada how strange it was that folks didn't mind seeing a woman's death so long as it seemed she was about to die.

By the end of the first hour, there was one and six on the paving slab in front of her. By the end of the second, she had just over five shillings in change and the man's death, if anything, looked larger than ever. There was more money to be had, Ada was sure, but with only a few minutes to spare, she picked up the coins from the ground and pocketed them, repairing to the bench before the man could return and discover that she had been profiting from his death. The seconds ticked by. Five past the hour. Ten past the hour. The darkness was drawing in, the blue-grey sky streaked through with the red of the setting sun.

Still the man did not return.

No matter, thought Ada, relishing the grip of agitation that squeezed ever tighter around her heart. He wouldn't be the first of her customers to return late. The longer he was delayed, the greater the satisfaction of relief would be when he finally returned.

But no sooner had she thought this than the man's death, his Yorick, up and bolted, barrelling away from her down the pavement at breakneck speed. Ada stared. A death flight like that meant only one thing.

The man was about to die.

She cursed. If the death found its man in the middle of a crowded restaurant, an apparently spare death peering sightlessly out from the panniers...She should never have allowed the trade. *Charlie* should never have allowed the trade, not with a man so close to the end. The signs had been obvious. In his condition, anything could have happened—a shock, perhaps, or even the sudden relief of having successfully pulled off his deception—and now he was dying.

Ada leapt to her feet and ran, weaving through the pedestrians with her skirts flying behind her, running in pursuit of the death as it bounded in the direction the man had gone more than two hours ago, past Sidney Sussex and, shortly after, past Christ's. The death did not stop or ease up for so much as a moment.

Then she felt it, like an unexpected blow to the stomach from an almighty fist, jolting her to a stand-still and seizing her lungs mid-breath. The hair on the back of her neck stood on end and her heart beat violently against her ribs. There was no mistaking that suffocating pain. How could he? How *dare* he?

But there was no time to think, for the death had not stopped running. Ada had never seen a death move so fast, its feet barely touching the ground as it raced on with spectral grace. It was all she could do to keep up. Her breath was coming hard and heavy with the effort and her legs burned. Still she ran.

Soon they had passed Emmanuel and then Ada could see Parker's Piece stretching out ahead, a shadow common in the twilight, the faint beam of the solitary lamp that stood at the centre doing little to dismiss the drawing darkness. Rather than bounding into the University Arms like she expected, the man's death bolted straight past the imposing edifice of white stone and marble pillars, and then carried on running, turning down the footpath that sliced through the heart of the Piece. Ada followed close behind, her boots pounding the compacted earth. She could barely see where she was going but she knew the footpath well and the darkness eased a little as she drew close to the solitary lamp at the crossroads that marked where the realm of the university ended and the domain of the city began. The lamp was known as the checkpoint and Ada passed it every time she came into town; the wrought iron as familiar to her as the knocker on her own front door. So she noticed at once the strange bulge of shadow where a figure slumped against the base of the lamppost. It was him. The dying man. And he was holding her death in his bare hands.

She snatched it away from him, lifting it up to cradle in her arms, stroking its fur and pressing it fiercely to her chest. Dizzying relief overwhelmed her. She clutched her death tightly, wild with the certainty of being once again whole. Then anger prised open her eyes and directed her attention to the man lying crumpled on the ground.

He had touched her death. Ada turned on him; spitting, snarling, half-ready to crash her boot into his ribs, keening to administer the same wrenching pain she'd suffered at his hands, too wild with fury to consider that in fleeing the restaurant the man may well have saved them both a great deal of trouble. But he didn't so much as glance at her, didn't seem to be even remotely aware of her presence, his eyes glassed over in the lamplight and focused on one thing only.

It happened quickly. He reached his arms out towards

his death, towards his Yorick, and the death threw back its head and gave a mighty howl that split the twilight. It was twice the size it had been a moment before and terrible to behold; no longer grey but a vivid, glimmering black, like a creature of living shadow. It leapt for the man, savaging him in an animal embrace that obscured him from sight. And then it was gone, dispersed, leaving nothing behind but a deathless corpse.

Ada fell back. For a long while, she stayed frozen to the spot and stared fixedly across the common, not daring to look down. The exhilaration of the chase and her fierce anger drained from her like the oozing pus of a blister that, when lanced, leaves behind nothing but a coin of loose, shrivelled skin, thin enough to tear at the slightest touch. She'd been sucked dry. Carved out. After all this time fantasising about the intensity of feeling that must accompany being party to real tragedy, and she wasn't sad or frightened or horror-struck. She wasn't anything. She was empty, as though bearing witness to the ultimate negating act had caused something in her to be negated also, and purged her of all sensation. No longer could she feel the cold tang of night or the ache in her legs. No longer could she see the vapour of each gasping breath or the shadows that closed about her. All else was still. For a moment the world became nothing and was populated by nothing, nothing but her and her death.

Then, at long last, she returned to herself. She came alive to the soft breeze grazing her lips, the slow throb of blood in the veins of her wrists and throat, the way the rough fabric of her underclothes lay against her skin. She swallowed hard. Gripping her death more tightly to her chest, she made herself look at the man's body.

There was something obscene about the staring, vacant eyes and how the skin seemed to become waxen and drawn in the yellow lamplight. She knelt beside the corpse and numbly closed its eyelids with her right hand. Then she straightened and tipped her head to one side, squinting as she tried to tell herself the man was only sleeping. But there was no escaping the absence at his side where his death should have lain. She tore her gaze away with a hollow cry, unable to bear the sight for another moment.

As if by way of reassurance, her own death flowed up her arm and curled itself around her neck. It felt heavier than before and she could see its bristling fur was streaked through with red. She knew instinctively that this alteration was permanent, brought about as much by bearing witness to the man's dying moment as by the deep physical stress of being molested, the small vulnerable thing hardening against the unsolicited touch of a stranger.

Ada shuddered and then reprimanded herself. It was what she wanted, wasn't it? For her death to grow and develop. She should be glad. If she was lucky, soon it would be large enough that she would no longer have to pretend suffering with the deaths of other men.

At just that moment, her death raised its head. Ada stared, her thoughts falling silent.

Then two new eyes flickered open to regard her. They were yellow with black slits notched across the centre; the feline eyes of a hunter.

Ada shuddered again. There was no doubting now whether her death was awake, not with those eyes patiently trained upon her. As if from nowhere, she found herself remembering the McLeever boy and his confusion at her evident delight upon being reunited with her death. It hadn't been like that for him. Nor for the rest of her customers, who were only restored to their deaths with the greatest of reluctance. She'd wondered at it often before. Now, at last, she thought she finally understood why; what it meant to possess a full-grown death, the horror that one might seek to contain, however ineffectually, with a joke or a name.

A knot in her heart tightened and this time, she realised, there would be no easy relief. In all her longing, she had never once imagined this dread, this fervent need to escape the watchful stare of her own death.

Philip Brian Hall

A Rainy Day at St Bartholomew's

The first raindrop landed, as if targeted, directly on Constable Smithers' head. He reached up absent-mindedly and, touching his thinning crown, felt a slight, unexpected dampness and thought nothing of it. Rain in London is hardly unusual, though generally Smithers was not hatless when out in bad weather. Sadly, a wetting was often required of him in the course of his police duties.

On this occasion, however, Constable Smithers' mind was on other things. Uncomfortably done up in best bib and tucker, he sat in the nave of London's oldest parish church, St Bartholomew the Great in Piccadilly. His carefully-brushed bowler was balanced awkwardly on the knees of his smartly-pressed trousers, a hymn book beside it preserving a precarious equilibrium next to brand-new kid gloves. His was the place of honour reserved for the best man.

In front of him and a little to his right was taking place

an event that would have been unthinkable mere months ago: the wily Old Red Fox of Scotland Yard, Sergeant MacAndrew, for so very many years a confirmed bachelor, had at last been brought to the altar. The lucky woman, if that could be considered the appropriate term, was Annie Quick, matron of The Royal London Hospital in Whitechapel. Smithers had never before encountered this formidable lady out of her nursing uniform, but he had to admit she made a lovely bride. She almost persuaded him to contemplate the alleged bliss of married life for himself.

It was as well that Annie had insisted on a short service with minimal ceremony. By the time that she and MacAndrew had signed the register and formally processed back down the aisle to their waiting carriage, heavy drops were steadily descending from several parts of the ceiling upon the progressively-dampening finery of the police officers and civic dignitaries assembled below. It appeared to be raining inside the Romanesque grandeur of St Bartholomew's as well as outside.

As soon as he'd seen off the happy couple, Smithers sought out the verger to find out what was going on. Reginald Childers was a short, red-faced man, inclining to stoutness and currently quite short of breath.

"I've been up to the clerestory, Mr. Smithers," he gasped. "I could hardly believe it. All the lead's been stripped from the roof of the aisles. Every ounce of it. I don't doubt the nave's the same. Completely open to the elements. It's a disaster! We'll have to get hold of some heavy canvas to provide emergency covering before the interior decoration's completely ruined."

"When could the theft have happened?" Smithers demanded.

"Last night," Childers replied, nodding vigorously. "It could only have been last night. I was around everywhere yesterday evening, making my usual inspection, as I always do before a big event in the church. There was absolutely nothing untoward."

"But we're talking about tons of lead here, man! How could thieves possibly steal so much in one night?"

"You're the policeman, Mr. Smithers." The verger shook his head sorrowfully. "I don't know, I'm sure. To show such terrible disrespect to the house of The Lord, though. I can hardly believe anyone could commit such sacrilege. May God strike down the wicked with His almighty hand, I say."

"Indeed," Smithers agreed. "But perhaps, in this particular case, I'll do some digging around and give The Lord a little assistance."

The typical London brewer's dray was a long, flatbed wagon with low, drop-down wooden sides, brightly-painted in the appropriate company livery and sporting a large wooden banner raised on poles at either end of the driver's seat, announcing to the world in ornate lettering the name of its proud owner. Typically drawn by two sturdy draught horses, matched bay Shires or chestnut Suffolk Punches, these drays might, upon occasion, carry as much as three full tuns, though since a tun held 216 gallons, weighed sixteen hundredweight and required a large crane to move, most pubs preferred to receive their ale supplies in more manageable one-eighth-of-a-tun barrels.

Around Shoreditch and Spitalfields, however, it seemed the local population must lately have developed a powerful thirst. Alerted to strange goings-on by one of his ubiquitous informants, Smithers stood staring goggle-eyed at a caravan of not one, not two, but three such impressive vehicles, each double-teamed by four straining horses, whose iron-shod hooves struck sparks from the cobbles as they met the slight gradient outside Truman's Brewery gates.

The wagons were piled high with pyramidally-stacked loads, consisting of quarter-tun hogsheads in ascending layers of five, four and three respectively. In the unlikely event that these contained beer, the loads were a good three tons each in weight. But as the three drays in turn struggled out of the brewery yard near Spitalfields Market, heading north, Smithers suspected they might be even heavier than that.

Recognising the leather-aproned driver seated high on the box of the first dray, Smithers called out to him. "Not you again, Fred Billings! I thought, the last time we met, you swore to mend your ways and lead an honest life!"

"And I 'as, Mr. Smithers, sir," the driver replied, his face rubicund in spite of his best efforts to sustain an image of calm. "See me 'ere, driving a brewer's dray, sir. Now you can't find more honest toil than that."

"I see you driving a brewer's dray, Billings, but I have my suspicions that those barrels do not contain beer. Where would you be bound now, seemingly with enough ale to float the entire Home Fleet?"

"Oh, you know, Mr. Smithers: Bethnal Green, then on to 'Ackney Marshes. They drinks a lot of beer up that way."

"So I hear, Billings. A good deal more than the inmates are allowed in Pentonville, I believe."

"Oh, now, Mr. Smithers, there's no call to talk that way. Just tell me what I can do to hassist your henquiries, sir, and I'll do it like a shot."

"For a start, Billings," Smithers growled, "You can pull up and let me examine those barrels."

Fitting his actions to the words, Smithers seized the

painted side of the flatbed and vaulted aboard the dray. He knocked firmly with a closed fist upon the end of the first hogshead. It emitted a dull clunk, as if tightly-packed with some solid such as flour or salt.

"If this barrel contains ale, or any other sort of liquid for that matter, Billings, I shall never impugn your honesty again," Smithers declared. "However, since it clearly doesn't, I don't think you're going to put me to shame, are you?"

Putting his whistle to his lips, Smithers blew three loud blasts.

Cometh the hour, cometh the man, they say, but Smithers was hardly expecting MacAndrew to be already present when he arrived at their shared office the next morning.

"She hasn't thrown you out already?" he enquired, only half-joking. The combination of MacAndrew and marriage had always seemed too good to be true.

"Not a bit of it," MacAndrew replied. "Annie considers forty-eight hours to be the maximum time she can possibly leave the denizens of The Royal London to their own devices. After that, the entire establishment would apparently go to Hell in a handcart."

"She is a very businesslike lady," Smithers agreed. "Since there are so few like her, she could well be right."

"Fortunately the same is not true of The Yard," said MacAndrew. "I gather in my absence you've been uncovering an outbreak of major crime?"

"Well, it's major in the sense of size at any rate," Smithers acknowledged. "I haven't yet established any connection between them, but the disappearance of tons of lead from the roof of St Bartholomew's and tons of sulphur from the gunpowder mills at Hounslow and

Dartford all seem to have occurred on the same night. It must have taken a veritable army of thieves. Strictly speaking, I suppose, whether it was one army or two remains to be established."

"You know what I think about coincidences," said MacAndrew. "You've interrogated Billings?"

"Yes. He coughed with very little encouragement. It seems the Hounslow and Dartford hauls were both transported to Spitalfields during the hours of darkness on the first night. They used local wagons for that, and then transferred the loads to Truman's drays for the next day's journey in an attempt to avoid arousing suspicion."

"Because the original drays would have been too far out of their regular delivery areas?" MacAndrew nodded.

"Just so. Billings and company surprised and overpowered the brewery's stable workers, leaving them bound and gagged, and stole the wagons and teams."

"You didn't find the lead with the sulphur, though?"

"Not yet. But I have all stations on the alert for heavy wagons. They won't get far."

"And where does Billings claim he was told to deliver the sulphur?"

"He's said Hackney Marshes right from the start. Nothing will shift him."

"There's not much up there," MacAndrew mused. "Paint factory at the old Temple Mills. Remains of the old powder mill that blew up towards the end of the last century. Ruins of Prince Rupert's armoury from the century before that." He paused. "But if the thieves wanted a quiet place to manufacture gunpowder for some nefarious purpose, why steal just sulphur and then transport it half-way across London? Why not steal ready-made gunpowder from the Hounslow and Dartford powder mills in the first place?"

"They must want the sulphur for some other reason," said Smithers. "But as far as I can see, the only raw material they can mix with sulphur in Hackney Marshes is water. There's plenty of that. The Lea floods regularly; there are stagnant ponds all over the place."

MacAndrew took out his pipe and filled it. Lighting up, he rose, strode over to the window and gazed out upon the street below. Smithers knew better than to disturb the ensuing silence. Finally, the Old Red Fox smiled.

"Let's assume the lead and the sulphur were stolen by the same gang," he said. "For the moment, I've no idea how they could mobilise the resources needed to mount even one of the robberies in the time available, let alone all three. But let's assume they did."

Smithers said nothing. He waited for the full idea to emerge.

"Have you heard of Gaston Planté, Smithers?" MacAndrew asked.

"Vaguely," the constable replied. "Something to do with electricity, isn't he? I remember reading about his work in a newspaper article a year or two ago."

"Back in 'fifty-nine, it was. He invented a method of storing electricity that could be used when no generator was available. He called it the lead-acid battery."

Smithers' eyes lit up. "I see, sir. And would the acid he used in his battery have been sulphuric acid by any chance?"

"It would."

"But surely, sir, these battery things will be quite small? If I remember rightly, wasn't it his idea that they should be portable? It makes no sense for thieves to suppose they could operate an illicit battery factory, without being detected, for long enough to use up so many tons of raw materials."

"Quite right, Smithers." MacAndrew's eyes twinkled. "But you and I have learned through experience that, these days, advanced scientific procedures can sometimes be very strange indeed. All this might make sense, for example, if, say, someone wanted to build a few giant batteries and use them where they're made."

"But are giant batteries even possible? And if they were, why on Earth would anyone want to do it, sir?"

"I've no idea, Smithers." MacAndrew smiled. "It's just a hypothesis."

As long as he was dealing with strangers, Smithers needed no disguise in order to pass for a street tough. The brawny physique and the broken nose of a pugilist came as part of the package, despite his middle-class upbringing and education.

Fred Billings swore the organiser of the robberies was a stranger to him. MacAndrew swore that if Billings turned out to be lying, and any harm came to his constable on account of it, Billings would find himself banged up in Shadwell nick faster than he could sink a draught of London gin. To the police, the old villain was of more use on the streets than inside a gaol, but it was still occasionally useful to remind him that, any time they wanted, they had him bang to rights on a certain recent charge of accessory to murder.

So it was that Smithers, bundled up in a shabby greatcoat, came to be sitting beside Billings on the driver's box of the first of the stolen Truman's drays approaching Hackney Marshes later that day. The wetlands loomed out of a thick mist that clung to the swampy surface; it was hardly possible to make out the rutted track they were following to the old powder works, let alone the scrubby trees that reached out their skeletal limbs at just the wrong height for such a large vehicle, scratching Smithers' unprotected face as the dray passed by.

The prevailing gloom had barely disclosed the shadowy outline of the ruin they sought, when a dark figure, a scarf wound around the lower part of his face, a broad-brimmed hat pulled down over his eyes, stepped out and confronted them.

"You're late!" the man snapped. "Where have you been? And where are the rest of the loads?"

"My sincerest hapologies, sir," Billings pleaded his excuses. "We 'ad a hunexpected run-in with the Peelers just past Spitalfields, sir. They seized all the wagons, an' impounded 'em back at Truman's, but I managed to get away, sir, and then last night me nephew 'ere an' me, we broke into Truman's an' stole one of 'em back, sir."

"Damnation! Are the other two drays still there?"

"Well, they was there last night, sir. As to this afternoon, sir, I'm afraid as I couldn't say."

"You should have had your nephew drive one of the others, idiot. What use is he sitting up there doing nothing?"

"I'm wery sorry, sir. But it seemed best to me to 'ave some hextra protection in case we met with a night-watchman, see."

The newcomer grumbled a reluctant assent. "All right. Take it around the back, out of sight from the road, and we'll unload. But this is not going to be enough sulphur. Somehow or other we're going to have to recover at least one more of the loads."

"Beggin' yer pardon, sir," said Smithers as they reached the rear of the ruins, where he was pleased to observe innumerable sheets of lead, already neatly stacked, "but ain't there no block an' tackle nor crane, sir? These 'ere 'ogs'eads is damnably 'eavy, see."

"Don't worry," the stranger said. "You won't have to exert yourselves. As you see, our ship lifted all this lead and brought it here. Unfortunately, we couldn't lift the sulphur too, because it was under cover in the powder warehouses. Now it's out in the open we can manage it."

Smithers looked all around him. In places, Hackney Marshes was wet enough to float a rowing boat, but it seemed improbable that the fog concealed anything larger. Nor, despite recent canal works on the Lea, was there any navigable river or other waterway connecting the marshes to St Bartholomew's.

"Ship, sir?" he enquired, genuinely perplexed.

"You don't need to know the details," the man said. "You do need to go back and get me another wagon load of sulphur and you need to do it quickly. We need everything in position by tomorrow."

"I can get you your sulphur," a quiet voice spoke from the fog behind them. "But I'm afraid I do need to know the details." A small figure emerged from the murk and then stood still. "Please don't be alarmed. Unless you intend to commit another crime, I mean you no harm."

"Who are you?" the man demanded.

"My name is Sergeant MacAndrew of Scotland Yard. You have already met Constable Smithers." MacAndrew pointed to his assistant. "As it happens, of all the policemen in London, we are the two most likely to believe you are not bent on a peculiar crime wave. Tell me, do you mean to recover the lead and return it after it has served your purpose?"

The stranger hesitated. Then he seemed to decide it might be better to trust MacAndrew rather than resort to other means. "Such was our plan, yes. Unfortunately, we shall not be able to return the sulphur. It must be chemically changed before use and the process is irreversible."

"You selected St Bartholomew's because it's one of London's few surviving Gothic churches and thus still had a lead-sheathed roof?"

"Correct."

MacAndrew smiled. "I must congratulate you on your command of English, sir. But I suspect it's not your native language. In fact, you probably learned it simply to assist in your present purpose."

"I did, yes."

"Then, Smithers," the sergeant turned to his constable, "I think that you and Billings should return to Spitalfields and fetch the other two drays. Take this one back there once it's unloaded and assure the brewery all three will be returned by this evening. If anyone objects, make clear you are acting on my authority and on a matter of national security. I'll remain here with our new friend. I hope we shall have a very interesting conversation while you're away."

The following day, half an hour short of noon, MacAndrew and Smithers descended from their cab in Hackney Wick and set out into the marshes on foot, following the same cart track. The weather was clear, so that, from a distance of over a hundred yards, they could already see a strange contraption poking up through the collapsed roof of the ruined powder mill. It resembled the perfectly-straight, tapering spout of a giant Regency coffee pot, save that it appeared to be of ceramic rather than metal construction. It was perhaps twenty feet high. From each of the four corners of the ruin rose shorter rods, each diagonally linked to the central spout by connections that suggested to Smithers an array of counting beads along the wires of some Brobdingnagian abacus.

The stranger met them a little further along the way. His face still obscured by scarf and hat, he was standing upon a wooden platform, raised about two feet above the ground and reached by four steps.

"Good day to you, gentlemen," he said.

"Hello again, Zinkar," said MacAndrew.

"You are in good time," the stranger acknowledged. "This is a safe distance, but even so, it is best not to be standing on the ground during the discharge. Please join me up here, and oblige me by putting on these dark glasses." He held out two pairs of spectacles towards them.

"You're confident there's no-one else nearby?" MacAndrew asked.

"Quite sure. We established a safety perimeter at the same time as we constructed the device. It would, of course, have been preferable if we could have brought everything we needed with us on our ship ready-assembled, but, as I told you yesterday, the mass and weight required were prohibitive."

"And where at this moment is this extraterrestrial rock of which you spoke?"

"The asteroid, as your scientist Herschel called such objects, is about fifty thousand of your miles away. Although it's two miles in diameter it's still too small to be seen by the naked eye."

"That seems very far away to be dangerous," said Smithers, dubiously.

"Bear in mind Earth is moving through space at sixty-six thousand miles per hour and the asteroid is approaching us at a similar speed," the man called Zinkar replied. "If we were to do nothing, the object would strike this very spot where we stand in a little over twenty minutes; the impact would cause an explosion sufficient to obliterate the whole of London and the home counties, killing millions immediately. It would leave a crater fifty miles wide and throw enough dust and debris into the atmosphere to block sunlight everywhere on Earth for decades, initiating a new Ice Age."

"Good Lord!" Smithers gasped.

"Small meteoroids hit your planet regularly," Zinkar explained. "They hit all planets, ours included. As a general rule, they land in seas or in uninhabited areas and do relatively little damage. We did not come all this way to help you avoid such minor inconvenience. We came to preserve life on Earth. In a few centuries, you will be able to join the trading community of civilised worlds, but, in order for you to do that, you must first survive."

"I suppose you couldn't undertake this work through official channels because the powers-that-be of our world aren't ready for such contact?" Smithers enquired.

"Correct. Sergeant MacAndrew has explained to me, however, that you, Mr. Smithers, have been able to introduce your fellow men to various other scientific novelties through the medium of detective-fiction stories." Zinkar made a sound that might have passed for a chuckle. "No doubt your leading authorities will describe today's events as an atmospheric phenomenon, but you will be able to tell people the truth because no-one will believe it. That is good. It is less frightening that way. Watch now. It is almost time."

As they turned their shaded eyes towards the strange machine inside the old ruin, a hum like the swarming of thousands of bees reached their ears. Gradually it increased in intensity until at last a dazzling flash broke from the ceramic spout and streaked skywards, as if a bolt of lightning had reversed the natural order of things by travelling from the ground to the heavens.

Moments later, a bright orange flare burst in the noon-day sky, spread widely, briefly outshining the sun and turning the tops of the scattered clouds to livid flame, before slowly dispersing and fading away into nothingness. A minute after that, all was as it had been before, as though the remarkable event had never occurred.

“That’s it?” Smithers enquired. “It’s all over?”

”For now,” said Zinkar. ”By the time the next troublesome meteoroid comes your way, we hope you’ll be in a position to deal with it for yourselves.”

“It seems somehow inadequate to say thank you,” MacAndrew mused.

“Never mind,” said Zinkar. “Let’s hope in a couple of hundred years’ time you’ll be able to make it worth our while.”

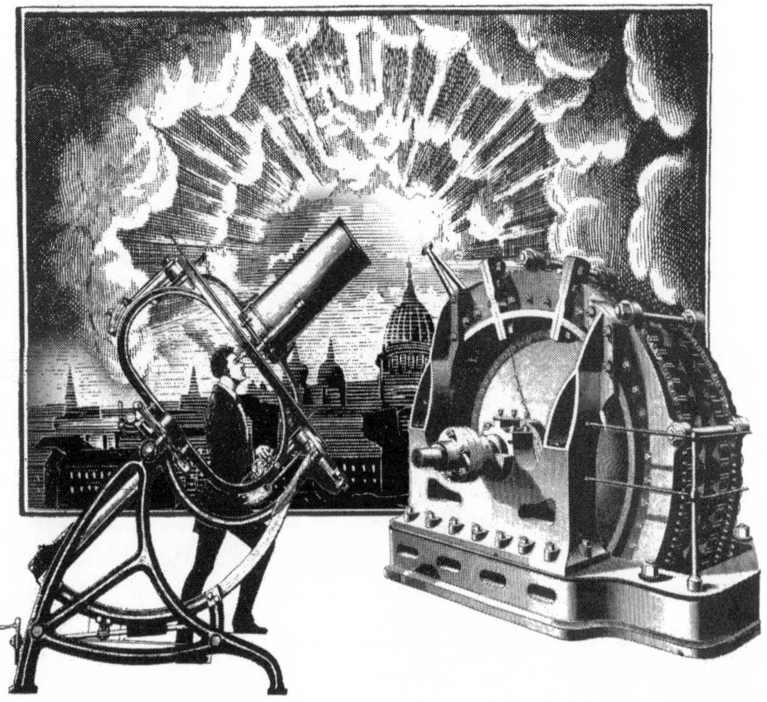

A.J. Brennan

Dorothea Defies Convention

My sister Violet says she doesn't give a fig for convention.

I tell her that in a village this size you must. If you slight, or startle, or scandalize anyone, they will still be talking about it in thirty years.

Violet says this is nothing to her. *She* intends to go and live in Paris as soon as the Monster Bonaparte is defeated. Taken up with this beguiling thought, she stops listening to me.

If she ever truly listened, I would tell her that while all ladies must consider their reputations, those that are magically inclined must be particularly careful. Neither Violet nor I is old enough to remember the witch burnings, but our grandmother told me of them and always reminded me to be grateful to the village for taking us in. We have been careful since then, and when the new laws came in and the new customs and conventions with them, we abided by them.

I also do not tell Violet that if you must defy convention, you should do it for something significant—something that will change your life forever—and be clear-eyed about the consequences. She must learn that for herself, as I did.

I send her to gather herbs in the garden, and she stalks off, with a muttered "Yes, Dorothea."

"If you plan to live in France, you should attend more to your French lessons!" I call after her.

I watch her for a moment from the doorway. It is a summer Monday morning, and the countryside is at its most lovely. The rain has stopped at last, and in the garden, the overgrown thickets of rosemary and thyme show the benefit of two weeks' downpour. Violet has forgotten her bonnet again, and she will have a freckled nose if she is not careful.

I feel so much guilt about what I am about to do. I cannot imagine how I will feel when I have actually done it.

Mother always said we were gentlewomen, and we are, more or less. After all, the vicar and the doctor are gentlemen, and what we do is somewhat like medicine and somewhat like religion. There is certainly Latin involved.

On most days, ladies from the village and the surrounding country come and have tea and aniseed cake and tell me about their husband's cough, or their daughter's fever, or their own troubled minds and sleepless nights. I nod and sip tea. When the visit is over, I give them something. Sometimes it is a powder or lozenges wrapped up in tissue paper crossed and re-crossed with words of power. Other times it is a tincture in a glass bottle engraved with minuscule writing. My visitors give me some silver in exchange, and if the price of the tea and cake is silently included, no one seems to regard it.

Other women come to the kitchen door, and I give them packets and bottles and do not charge them for the tea. More rarely, messengers come from London and as far away as York.

I considered setting up in London after mother's death, but the living is cheap here, and our carefully maintained reputation shields us. When I look around at what I have built these last ten years, I am proud.

Nevertheless, I am conscious of how quickly the years between eighteen and twenty–eight have passed: one headache powder, one throat pastille, one sight-restoring tincture at a time. The gossip and symptoms I hear tomorrow will be much the same as today's, which were much the same as yesterday's. It would be impolite to show boredom, though I have heard them all before.

I know that I should not wish for change. Change could only be dangerous to us. I know that I should be grateful for all of the good things, and not struggle too much against the restrictions.

We are invited to the Great House every month for dinner, which is an honor, if not always a pleasure. Sometimes, when they are truly desperate for company, we are invited twice in a month. We are also invited to tea at the vicarage every Saturday. The new vicar is broad-minded, and likely does not burn incense to ward off evil spirits when we leave.

On Sundays, I arrange the church flowers with the rest of the Ladies' Altar Guild. They make conversation about husbands and children. I talk about the garden and the weather, and listen to their stories politely for the fourth or fifth time.

Every day I watch Violet and worry about her future. I

never spare a thought for my own, until, one day, I receive a letter from Colonel Fitzhugh.

I know Colonel Fitzhugh a little. His family has always lived in the Great House, and he returned there to recover after he came back from the colonies with a ball in his shoulder. I visited with my mother to administer spells and change the dressings on the wound. After she fell ill, I came alone. On some nights, if I had a few spare minutes, I would read to him from histories of great Roman generals that bowed his bookshelves. His sister, there to chaperone, always nodded off during the battles.

My good command of Latin surprised him more than my indifference at the sight of blood, or my willingness to come alone to tend to him. I explained that I was the one who said the words of power over the powders and inscribed the necessary phrases on their wrapping.

This shocked him a little, although I do not know who else he imagined could have been doing it. There were only the three of us—mother was sick in bed, and Violet was only five.

In time, he healed. The muscle and bone mended so completely that you could not tell he had ever been injured. He returned to the Army, and I heard of him only occasionally through his mother and sister.

This spring, he wrote to me from the battlefield and asked if I knew any strong healers fit for military service. Casualties had been heavy, and they needed additional men. I replied, telling him that I did. He was resistant, of course, but we both knew that few men are as skilled as I, and those who are had already gone to the Continent. We both remembered his own shoulder and that when his father was thrown from a horse and broke his skull, they sent for me, and the old lord lived. In the end, the Colonel accepted my offer.

I cannot help but wonder if he had always hoped that I would propose myself. Why else write to me, after all?

* * *

On Tuesday, Violet discovers me in the stillroom, making packet after packet of healing powders. I had made certain she would be out and given Ellen the afternoon off to ensure that I could work privately, but Violet has caught me out.

I have prepared dozens of remedies, properly bespelled to stop bleeding, knit fractured bone, and mend torn flesh. I have copied the instructions out neatly in a small notebook, light enough to carry, but I must also carry them at the front of my mind and the tips of my fingers. Perhaps I will need to make them on a battlefield. Teas for easing pain and curing fever I can already make without pausing to think.

I do not know what to expect. All that I can do is prepare everything I know how and hope that that will be enough. I have seen broken bones and torn flesh before, and there have been people I have not been able to save. Not many, but some. I do not know if this prepares me to go to war.

When Violet comes in, the work table is so covered in little paper packets that some have slid to the floor. The scent of the powders is pungent and not altogether pleasant, so I have opened the window to catch the breeze. I am at the window looking out when I hear her come up behind me. I spin around guiltily.

She was supposed to have been picking berries, and she is carrying a basket with some berries in it, but I notice that she is also wearing one of her finest dresses, and she looks a little too pleased with herself.

I hope she has not been meeting with Tom from the Red Farm. He is a nice lad and perfectly respectful, but I know that a romance between them cannot end happily. Whatever social advancement our tenuous gentility can offer him, his family would not allow him to unite himself to one of us.

I hope that Violet has taken my hints about this, and she will not force me to be blunt. That would wound us both. Since I do not wish to have that conversation, I do not ask her about the dress.

Violet turns over one of the packets, reading my tiny careful writing. She reads another. "This one is to mend broken bones, and this one is to heal wounds to the heart or lung," she says.

So she has been listening, to my lessons if not my lectures.

She raises her eyebrows at the heap of spells. "What kind of disaster are you expecting?" she asks.

"There is no harm in being prepared," I say, sweeping the packets off the table and into a basket.

She seems to believe me and to put this behavior down to my usual fussy ways. Why should she not believe me? Until these last few weeks, I never lied to her.

Perhaps I could simply tell her my plan. It would be such a relief to me to do so. I know, however, that if she asks me to stay I will. More likely, she would ask to come with me, and I might not have it in me to tell her no. She is too young to understand the consequences of such a choice, and she might yet learn to live and be happy here. That would surely be best for her.

On Wednesday, I visit the sick. I give each of them enough spells for two weeks. If anyone notices this precaution, they do not remark on it. For most of them, the powder or tincture itself is sufficient, but for those who require an additional spell to be said over them, I have left very specific instructions. Violet knows quite well what to do and does not need my reminders, but it comforts me to write them down.

In each house, I sit and talk a little, as I do on every visit, though perhaps a bit longer than I would any other week. By the end of the day, I have drunk more tea than two women could could hold, and I slosh home. I do not tell anyone I am leaving, and, except in the ordinary way, I do not say goodbye.

Finally, on Thursday, three days after my last lecture on propriety, I am packing a bag in the middle of the night, knowing that I am a hypocrite. I have already sent a letter to our aunt, asking her to come down and stay with Violet, I imagine she will be eager enough to leave her grim seaside boarding house.

Violet believes she can look after herself, but she is only fifteen and not careful, and what I am doing will make things so much more difficult for her.

I leave the second letter, the one for Violet, on the hall table. I had written her a letter of warnings: do not set your heart on Tom from the Red Farm. Always be seen at church on Sunday. Never be hasty, or high-handed, or careless, or rude. Be careful. Then, I tore it up and wrote her a letter full of love.

I hope she will forgive me, and I hope that one day, I will be able to apologize face-to-face, even if I can never come back here again.

I step out onto the path. The coach that will take me to Calais is waiting at a posting house on the main road. I asked that it wait there, although it does not matter now if anyone sees me. The night does not frighten me. I have a pocketful of very noxious spells for anyone or anything I might meet along the way.

I expect that His Majesty's generals will not much welcome me when I arrive, but I must go. Such an opportunity may never come my way again. Military service is my chance to see the world, yes, but, most importantly, it offers the safety of a government post, with no taint of hedgewitchery about it. I will have room to breathe at last.

I look back. The house is Violet's now, and perhaps that will weigh in the balance with Tom's family. Perhaps, when the war ends, she will forget him and go to Paris.

Then I see Violet standing in her lit window. She stares down at me and sees the valise in my hand. After a moment, she waves, and I understand that she is urging me onward.

Harris Coverley

The Instant

After our game of cards had ended, Hemming placed the box on the table and explained its purpose: "It's a kind of stimulator, a means to experience an emotion you otherwise have a hard time grasping for yourself."

"Yes, but does it work?" asked Ashberry, obviously not swallowing the premise, and more concerned at that moment with counting his ample winnings.

"Nobody really knows," replied Hemming, repositioning the box a little further from the table's edge. "The inventor died decades ago and it was not found until years after his death, in his storage space, with instructions stuck to its side. All you have to do is lift the lid, stick your head in and ask what you want to experience. It's quite a fun little thing...if you're in the mood that is?"

We were all quite in the mood as a matter of fact, the

brandy having loosened us and the night being soaked with warm dew pouring from the open window that filled the air with sweetness and vigour.

Ashberry, the sceptic, volunteered himself for the first try.

The box itself was of a uniform rectangular construction, carved from some unusually streaked wood from the Far East, Malaya or somewhere like that, but it otherwise seemed unremarkable, rising some eight inches tall, and being roughly ten inches by eight in perimeter.

Hemming, from his seat, slid off the lock-free lid with ease, and instructed Ashberry to stand up and insert his head into the box. Ashberry took a quick sip of his drink before doing as Hemming requested, leaning his hands on the table and gingerly sticking his face into the box.

"Your whole head," Hemming said, "what I was told anyway, or else it might not work properly."

Ashberry lifted his face back out to look at his host: "Where did you acquire this thing anyway?"

"Part of a lot at auction last week...a blind bid on knick-knacks and whatnots. Some good, some dubious, but all interesting nonetheless...go on, insert your whole head."

Hemming smiled with a playful wickedness.

Slowly, Ashberry lowered his head into the box, until it was submerged utterly and we felt his forehead touch the base.

"Now what?" Ashberry asked.

"Ask it for which emotion you want," Hemming said, a tighter grip on his glass betraying anticipation. "Something you have trouble experiencing...anything."

There was a pause, before Ashberry's voice echoed out of the box: "I ask for joy."

There was some giggling amongst us, and I admit I joined in. Hemming hushed us, but it was only a moment before we could see results.

Ashberry raised his body up, not in shock or pain, but

in abject elation. He walked about the room laughing, with so much happiness I thought this usually dour acquaintance had become possessed.

After a few minutes his big smile remained, but he calmed down enough to sit in his chair and get back to his brandy. A little while later, he had gained enough measure of self-control to explain himself: "It was so wonderful! It was like being free of all dread...I hadn't felt so marvellous since I was a young boy, frolicking with my father's hounds in the woods!"

Ashberry soon became too exhausted to continue any conversation, and was led by Hemming's butler to the guest room to lie down for a time, maybe even a night.

After such a display any residual scepticism in the room had dissipated, and we were all eager to give the box a try.

Hemming, not wanting to play favourites, decided to utilise some matches in hand to see who could win the next go by lot. The remaining five of us drew and I received the shortest match, traditionally reserved for the delegation of an unpleasant task, an irony not lost on me in retrospect.

I did as Ashberry had done before me: I stood straight in front of the open box, leaned my hands on the table at either side, and inserted my head entirely inside. I stood there like some deranged emu-man for a moment, before remembering the need for a verbal request, which, with little thought, I gave: "I wish for love."

My body tensed in expectation for a rush of emotion like that of Ashberry's experience, but as the seconds mounted, nothing came to pass, and after nearly a minute of posing a crick in my neck began to develop and I had to stand straight, to the sight of five disappointed faces whom had expected a show.

"Well?" asked Hemming, his glass refilled.

"Nothing," I said, sitting back down. "No sensation, no impressions…no love."

The sombreness of my words blunted what remained of any excitement, and we sat in silence for a while, nursing our drinks, and watching the grandfather clock reach eleven.

I broke the hush: "Hemming, what is the name of this thing anyway?"

"It has no name," he replied, looking at the box mournfully. "It came with none in the lot, and the inventor, rest his soul, left none, or at least that's what the auction house people told me. Until your misfortune, due to the box's efficiency and promptness, I was tempted to call it something like 'The Instant', but to the devil with that now…"

"Maybe it just doesn't prefer you?" said Cartwright, a stuffy little man who dealt in fabrics, and with whom I'd had strong words with in the recent past.

It was then decided that I should repeat the entire procedure, which I did, but after yet another minute with my head in the box after my wish was made, I arose unfulfilled, and the rest of the guests and my host fully disillusioned. It was quickly agreed that the evening's festivities would come to an end.

"Do not worry," Hemming told me at the door as I fitted my top hat, "I'm sure it was just a gremlin in the works. When we meet here again in a fortnight, we'll have another go, and have a good gay time."

I thanked him for his hospitality, bade him and his butler holding the door a good night, and went down to my waiting carriage, the last to depart.

The journey from Hemming's house to my own is a swift one, and long before midnight I was in my hallway, my maid taking my coat and hat, and me deciding to have

a nightcap in the lounge. I had the rest of the weekend to enjoy in relative solitude.

I poured a small whiskey in a silver goblet and sat in my armchair before the empty fire, grateful in the knowledge that the maid was making my bed.

A Miss Florence Holt, whose origins lay in the North, to me she was still a young girl, not yet thirty years, and in my service for the past five. She was a great asset, a tremendous woman…wonderful…beautiful…very forgiving of an old fool like me…

As I swallowed my liquor these thoughts began to dominate my mind, thoughts which had never before come to pass. Within minutes I found myself totally enraptured, my bachelor attitudes dissolved, and the passion of an insane Don Juan taking hold of me. I was suddenly madly in love with Miss Holt, and nothing could dissuade me otherwise. Reason abandoned me absolutely.

She soon came in to tell me that my bed was ready, and, struck with that passion, I compelled her to sit down and join me in a drink. She was extremely confused with this turn, never having been involved in any aspect of my personal affairs before.

She sat awkwardly on the divan next to my chair as I poured her a whiskey, and myself another to the top of the rim. Before giving her the drink, I swigged half of mine down in one go, and soon found myself, this disease overpowering what remained of my senses, on my knees before Florence, stroking and kissing her hand, confessing how much she spontaneously meant to me. Confusion on her face gave way to terror, and she made to get up, her drink spilling. I rose up and forced her down, tearing her white apron. She struggled as my mouth moved over her quivering lips. She began to fight me and scream. I tore more of her uniform, as, I confess in disgrace, I began to remove my own clothes in the process.

She kicked and bit and scratched, and with a well-aimed knee to my chest finally broke from my grip and ran out of the lounge. Briefly stunned, I managed to get to my feet and give chase as I heard the front door swing open, and her little feet, her precious, tiny feet, fly out into the street.

For half-a-dozen streets I ran within inches of her, both of us taking on Hermean speed, me in inexplicable lust, her in virginal horror. Soon a crowd, attracted by all the tumult, followed us and closed in on me, a gang of men holding me down until the police arrived to carry my person, crippled by desire, to a cell.

A day later I was dragged before a judge and was ruled insane, but thanks to the intervention of a family friend, was saved from the asylum and placed under the care of a doctor on Harley Street. It took two months of intense and psychically painful alienism, isolated from the rest of the world of news both public and private, but I gradually lost my love for poor Miss Holt, who had been ferried back North to her family with a sizeable endowment for her cooperation and silence.

The doctor insisted that my psychosis had been brought on by the stress and isolation of my work, but as soon as I was permitted to leave his care I made my way to Hemming's house to discuss the effects of that infernal box of his, hoping to see the damned thing burned before the day was out.

I arrived late in the afternoon to find his house empty, the furniture covered, and the butler packed and preparing to leave for the last time.

"What is all this?" I asked him, looking quite pale and emaciated from my long treatment, convulsing in the approaching Autumn chill. "Where is Mr Hemming?"

The butler matched my paleness: "He is dead sir."

Somehow part of me knew that was already the case, but I was devastated regardless. The butler was kind enough to let me in and uncover a chair for me to sit on.

He explained to me: "It happened over a month ago. A week ago his family sold his house and I'm leaving today for new employment."

"Why sell the house so quickly?" I asked.

"For the shame sir," he replied.

"The shame?"

"Yes, Master Hemming, I'm afraid, hung himself, sorry to say from that very chandelier there," said the butler, and pointed to the light high above the stairway across from the landing.

"But why?" I asked, struggling to accept it.

"He heard about you sir," the butler said, "he understood immediately that it was his 'Instant' as he called it, and decided to try it again. He asked for something he wanted, and within an hour he had done the deed."

"What happened to the box?"

"I don't know sir; when they cleared the house of smaller articles it got swept-up with the rest. I told them to destroy it, but I'm sorry to say I was discounted."

Drained of any strength, I decided to leave for home and attempt to put my own affairs in order. As we were making our way down the porch steps, the butler with his travelling case in hand, I asked him, "Do you know what Mr Hemming asked the box for?"

"Yes sir," he said, "I was there."

"What was it then?"

"Peace, sir."

As of writing, no one has recovered the box, and I hope that forever remains the case for any living soul.

JL George

Shards

he first time Else appeared, in the old parlour on the second floor of the House, she descended from the glass like an angel from the heavens.

The angle of the mirror warped her image and made her appear huge, so that for a second Red feared she wouldn't see him and he'd splinter beneath her foot like a rotten beam. She wore a necklace of crystal points, each one like a tiny dagger at rest against her collarbone, and at the moment she appeared a beam of sunlight hit the mirror glass so it seemed she had a burst of light in place of a head.

When Red was small, after Mother had died and before the House, he and his older brother had crept into an abandoned chapel to sleep out of the rain. Aled had prayed for the angels to keep Mother safe in Heaven, and

Red had found a strange old book and looked at the pictures of them—monsters of unearthly, unceasing fire with bodies full of eyes. He'd dreamed about angels that night and woken screaming, and afterward Aled had hidden the book and hadn't prayed any more.

The angels in his dream had looked like this: explosions of light frozen mid-blast. He gazed up wide-eyed, unable to move.

Then Else jumped down from the mantel, dusted off her skirt, and regarded him with big, frank brown eyes. "Who are you?" she demanded, and then, as though remembering to do so was a bit of an inconvenience, added, "I'm Else."

"Red." He stuck out his hand, because that was what you did when you were trying to be polite. Nobody in the House really bothered, of course, but something about Else made him feel he should make the effort. Her clothes were blindingly clean, for one thing, and he couldn't see a single patch or darned-up tear. Perhaps that meant she was important.

"Red." She repeated it as though tasting a spoonful of something unfamiliar and finding herself uncertain that she liked it. "Strange name. And you're not even ginger."

In fact, the nickname had been bestowed by Aled shortly after he was born, his brother having squinted at his bawling, screwed up face and inquired why he looked like a squashed tomato. "I thought babies were supposed to be cute," he'd said. "Not all red and stuff."

It had stuck, though after the initial shock of birth Red hadn't been much given to ruddy-faced screaming, and Mother had repeated the story to them many times before she died. He remembered that, but fuzzily, the image of her telling the story blurring around the edges and overlapping with all the times Aled had recited it.

Red didn't share any of that, though, just rubbed at the

back of his neck. "Well," he admitted, "I suppose this is a bit of a strange place." Not to him, particularly, but definitely to the outsiders who pressed their faces up to the gaps in the fence, or even strolled right up to the front door to gawp.

Was Else an outsider or an insider? She'd come through the looking-glass, after all, and all he saw through it now was a reflection of the room in which he stood.

Outsider or not, Else perked up. "Are you going to show me around?"

The House wasn't the sort of place you showed people around, Red didn't think. It was the sort of place you crept into quietly, as he and Aled had years ago with their worn-thin shoes and skinny limbs. You found a corner and, piecemeal, borrowed and begged yourself a life until you were woven into the fabric of it, its peeling gold paint and crumbling spiral staircases and the diamond-shaped lattices where windowpanes had once been, and where you now had to keep out the wind with old blankets or pieces of wood, or if you were particularly unlucky, your backside.

Once you'd been here long enough you became part of the House—like Old Cath, who rarely moved from her corner and sometimes got mistaken for a piece of the furniture, the blue curl of smoke from her pipe the only thing giving her away. There were faces carved above doorways and mantels and in the corners of ceilings, and some of the inhabitants whispered that they'd once been people, too, calcified into the bricks and mortar of the House over decades.

Else was looking at him eagerly, the sunlight shining in her eyes and the stones on her necklace. They glittered; Red found his magpie-eyes darting to them. You could probably swap one of those crystal shards for *months'* worth of food. Perhaps she might give him one as a thank-you, if she was pleased.

"Alright," said Red, and cleared his throat. "Follow me."

Else delighted at the fountains shaped like fish in the front garden, though they were broken and gave out no water, only a cracked whistling note when the wind played over them. She crawled into the cobwebby spaces behind the walls as though it meant nothing to catch her skirts on nails and find spiders in her golden hair. She petted the tame rat that Aled had taught to guard their meagre food store with a fierce nip, and gave an affronted yell when it drew blood from her thumb.

She drew a trail of curious admirers—or gawkers, anyway—from all over the House and Red basked in the reflected glow, feeling chosen, though it was only chance that had dropped Else at his side.

The sun sank outside and the House began to curl in on itself for the night, residents finding their corners and cubbyholes, lighting lamps and candles. Else glanced up, surprised, at the nearest window, and then stretched lazily.

"I suppose I should be getting back," she said. "I'll be late for my supper." And then she gave Red a secretive smile, one that made him feel they were co-conspirators. "Come back to the parlour with me. You might be able to see through to the other side."

Red held his breath before the mirror, exhaling in disappointment when it showed only his own face, the room in which they stood, and Else's pale reflection like a waxen figure beside him. The fiery light of sunset flooded in through the window, and for a moment he expected her to melt.

Else's sharp elbow found his ribs, then, and she smirked up at him. "You can't just look through the mirror and see it, stupid," she told him. "You have to do it properly."

With a flourish, she plucked one of the shards from her necklace and flicked it with the white tip of a fingernail. The note that rang out was bright and clear and too loud for the tiny shard it had come from. It resonated inside Red's ears and the bones of his skull, making his head swim, and the plain glass of the mirror seemed to swim with it too, growing unsettled like the water in the garden pond when a breeze disturbed it.

And then it stilled, and the ringing in his head faded, and he saw.

The mirror showed the room they were standing in, but different. The iron lattices in the windows were paned with glass, a different coloured square in each diamond, so the sunlight made the whole room a shining rainbow. The furniture, all intact, had been polished until the wood seemed to glow from within, and plump pillows and soft blankets lay on every chair. A low table held bone-pale china cups and a teapot, and a silver tray laden with sandwiches—delicate triangular ones made from bread as white and soft as clouds, which surely couldn't have made for more than a single bite. There were apples, too, and cherries, and little dome-shaped cakes with pink icing on top. In a basket near the door, a white cat snoozed with one paw tucked over its nose.

It was the strangest and most beautiful thing Red had ever seen.

"There's no need to stare," Else told him, "it's only my parlour." *(Her* parlour. How strange, to think so spacious a room could belong to only one person.) But there was something pleased in her expression, and Red thought perhaps she'd meant to impress him.

"Can I come with you?" he found himself saying. "See your world, like you saw this one?"

Else looked regretful. Genuinely so, he thought. "I

wish you could," she said. "But I've tried, before. To bring people with me. It didn't go so well."

Red opened his mouth to ask what she meant, but she was already clambering up onto a chair. She waved to him and stepped through the mirror, and behind her it shimmered and turned again to solid glass.

Red waited for her without quite knowing he was waiting.

Before she appeared, he'd been content enough with the House, its labyrinthine passages and homey corners and kingdoms the size of a room, a landing, a cupboard. But when Else had vanished through the mirror, it had felt like seeing a window shuttered. He grew sulky and distracted. Aled needled him about having his head stuck in the attic. More often, though, he was in the parlour, gazing at the mirror, hoping for the glass to ripple and for Else to emerge like a fussy-frilled Venus from the waves.

A week passed, and another, and she didn't come back. He began to give up.

Then, in the dead of night, in the dead of sleep, Red was jolted into consciousness by a hand shaking his shoulder. It was a rough awakening: the kind that left his heart rabbiting and his eyes wide with terror, even as the dream he'd been having clung hazily to his mind. It had been a bad one. He'd been swimming, but the water had turned slurry-thick and strands of golden hair had wound themselves around his ankles and held him fast.

"Wakey wakey!" Else whispered, too close to his ear, in the dark.

She was bright-eyed and full of energy, agog to see the night-time sights of the House. Red sloughed off his sleepiness as best he could and led her to the grounds, where the fish in the crumbling pond glowed golden and danced with the reflection of the moon, and night-blooming flowers woke among the beds of weeds and breathed out their fragrances in the dark.

Else tilted her head and inhaled, smiling, then looked to Red. "Where next?"

He blinked and looked around. Everywhere else in the House inhabitants drowsed. There would be no exploring without clambering over somebody's bed. He said as much.

"Oh." Else looked slightly put out. "Well, I can't wait 'til morning. I have to get back home before Mother wakes up."

They tried feeding the fish with berries plucked from among the weeds. Those were roundly rejected. They played four-in-a-row by moonlight with dark and light pebbles from the garden, until Else got bored and curled up to doze on the lawn. Soon enough Red grew drowsy and stretched out beside her to resume his interrupted sleep.

When the first rays of sunlight touched his face and woke him, Else was gone. Red scrambled to his feet and tore up to the parlour just in time to hear a ringing note fade into silence, the surface of the glass stilling like water after a stone is dropped into it.

Something lay on the floor before the fireplace. Red stooped to pick it up and found it cold in his hand. A shard of crystal from Else's necklace, smooth along the sides and knife-sharp at the points, and clear as an icicle.

He slipped it into his pocket. It did not warm with the heat of his body, and every time he remembered it was there excitement curled in his gut, as though he held the key to a secret world.

He didn't know how it worked, of course. That was the problem. Else had made it sing with a single flick of her fingernail, but when Red tried it, the only sound he elicited was a dull tap. He didn't dare ask her the next time she appeared, though, for fear she'd demand her shard of crystal back and he'd be shut out of the possibility of seeing her world once more.

When they were small and hiding, before the House, Aled had stolen food for them from a market stall around the corner from the chapel. He'd said it wasn't wrong, because the market trader had enough to eat *and* to sell, and they had nothing. Well, Else had enough crystals to open a dozen mirrors, and Red had never even touched one before.

He kept it from Aled, though. He was fairly sure his brother wouldn't think it was the same.

He walked with Else to the parlour the next time she decided to go home, and watched carefully the movement of her hand and the angle of her wrist when she struck that one bright note from a shard on her necklace.

When she'd gone and the mirror had settled, Red looked around him to make sure no-one was watching and pulled his own piece of crystal from his pocket. Carefully, he imitated Else's motions, the single controlled flick of her finger.

This time, a thin clear note rang out from the crystal shard. Red watched the mirror breathlessly as its surface stirred—not much, just as though it were liquid and he'd exhaled on it. His breath caught as the image wavered; gave the barest hint of a warm red glow, as of the fireplace in that other parlour, in Else's world.

It settled, then, and Red's own face looked back at him, mouth downturned and sulky. For a moment he caught a glimpse of the screaming baby Aled had nicknamed, and the thought flushed him with embarrassment.

He breathed in deeply, watching the mirror until he looked calm once more.

"It's beautiful," he said to her, once, gesturing at the necklace. He hoped she'd open up about it, he supposed, let slip some clue as to how the crystals worked.

Else nodded, accepting the compliment as her due.

"But they're all different colours," Red pressed. "The —the jewels, or whatever they are."

At that, Else's expression stiffened minutely. "Yes," she said. "They are."

"Did you collect them from different places? Or were they presents?" Seeing the still line of her mouth, then, he blinked and looked down. "Er, sorry if I'm being nosy. I just—I'm not used to seeing things like that, I suppose."

"It's alright," she told him, softening. "No, they're not presents, exactly." She ran her fingertips over the shards like the keys of a piano. One held the faintest tint of honey-gold; another the blue of a pale winter's sky. Another green, like a painting he'd once seen of the Northern Lights. "They just—remind me of different people, that's all."

"Oh?" said Red, but Else didn't look at him. After a moment she raised her eyes.

"Let's explore the attic!" she said. "I haven't been there yet. I bet there are loads of things to see."

The next time Else left, he didn't wait for the mirror to settle before striking a note out of the crystal.

Through the mirror, he saw the warm room again. This time the white cat was nowhere to be seen, but balls of wool unspooling across the armchair betrayed its presence. Else didn't stop to ravel them up again but made for the door, her back to the mirror.

She stopped before she got there. Another figure appeared in the doorway, and Red hunkered down instinctively, peering over the bottom of the mirror, heart hammering.

It was a woman with Else's golden curls—though she wore them pinned up atop her head—wearing a long blue dress. She laughed and caught Else by the shoulders with her white hands. "There you are!" she said. "Where have you been?"

Else tossed her head, careless. "Oh," she said. "Nowhere."

Of course she couldn't tell. Her mother might take the mirror away, and then Red would never see her or the strange other world again. It still made him wince a little to hear how easily the lie came. His grip tightened on the crystal shard—and its note died away, dampened. The surface of the mirror shimmered and stilled and Red was alone with his reflection again.

That night he dreamed of his own mother. He didn't have many memories of her, really—just her pinched, worried face and her stringy black hair, and her telling that same story over and over. Her hands had been gentle, though. That stayed with him.

Aled remembered her better than Red did. That was why he'd prayed for her, Red supposed, back in the chapel where they'd hidden and where he'd found the book of angels.

There had been an image on one page that made Red want to turn over fast so he wouldn't see it, and then made him look back, inching the pages apart little by little as though to keep it from seeing him. It had had so many eyes, after all, and it had burned all over with white fire and worn a crown of icy shards.

What kind of a song would those shards have sung? What kind of a door might they have opened?

* * *

"I don't know why you spend all your time with that outsider girl," Aled told him. It was night, and they drank their mugs of soup sitting with their backs against the cold wall of the House.

Red scowled, defensive. "Else's nice."

"I'm not saying she isn't." Aled sighed. "Just—don't go getting ideas, that's all. She's not like us. She's not from here."

"No," said Red, "she's not," and stared down into his soup until Aled left it alone. The crystal in his pocket burned coldly against his leg, and that night, when Red closed his eyes, he imagined he heard it singing to him.

* * *

The next time Else came and went, he was lucky. She'd scooped up the cat and tripped out of the door before the mirror settled. Heart in his throat, Red drew the crystal shard from his pocket.

The note he struck from it rang out sonorous and pure. The surface of the mirror stilled, and through it he saw Else's world, sharp and bright as if he could reach out and touch it.

Perhaps he could.

Red grabbed one of the chairs stacked up against the parlour wall and clambered onto it, the fraying brocade giving beneath his feet. He clutched at the mantel to hold himself steady, and stood fully upright on shaking legs.

Then he reached out.

The mirror felt like ice water, the cold shock of it making him draw back his hand at the first touch. He bit his lip, steeled himself, and raised his hand once more.

The surface gave. Red pushed a little further, tilting precariously forward on the chair. He held his breath.

Something pulled at him, then. A current, a whirlpool, a wind, the surface of the mirror reaching for him like the waves of a cold sea. Red tried to jerk back. He couldn't.

He was falling forward now, into the chill implacable depths of the mirror, and it was freezing around him, immobilizing arms and legs. He tried to call out for Aled but his voice was frozen too, it was solid in his throat and he was choking on it. Dark spots danced before his eyes. He felt his feet leave the chair, and then all was black and cold.

The surface of the mirror was quite still when Else returned to the parlour. She frowned, glancing around the room. The cat had stiffened and yowled and jumped from her arms, unsettled the way it always was when she used the mirror. Otherwise she never would have guessed someone had been interfering with it.

It took her a moment to notice. There, before the fireplace, glimmering in the light of the flames.

Two shards of crystal. The one she'd noticed missing from her necklace a couple of days ago—and another, faintly pinkish in hue. Or—no, not pink. Red.

When she pinged it with her forefinger, it made a sound like a cry of fright.

Else frowned at it. Why did they never listen to her?

"Else!" Mother, calling from down the corridor. "Supper!"

She sighed, slotted both shards into her necklace, and made for the dining-room. Perhaps there would be apple cake this evening.

MM Schreier

Inked

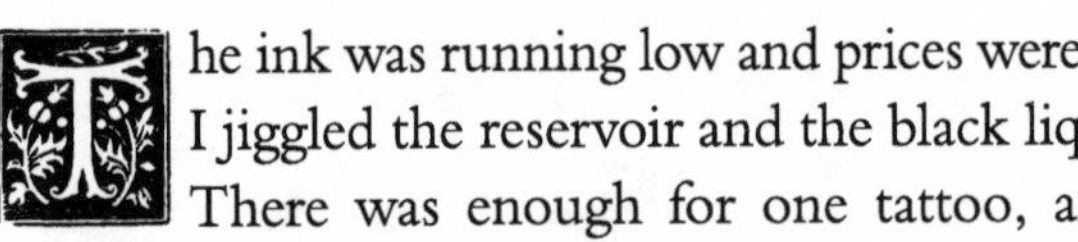

The ink was running low and prices were outrageous. I jiggled the reservoir and the black liquid sloshed. There was enough for one tattoo, and then I'd need more. If I could scrape up the coin. The rent was due yesterday, and I had pretended I wasn't home when the landlord knocked. I sighed and tugged a lever. The sudden hiss of steam made Viktor jump.

"Are you sure that contraption is safe, Augustus?"

I rolled my eyes. "Of course it is. State-of-the art. Designed it myself."

He didn't look convinced. "That's what I'm afraid of."

With his bulging muscles, it seemed ridiculous that the bruiser was afraid of a few pipes and whirling gears. Viktor shifted in his seat and it creaked.

If you break my only chair, Vik, I'll kill you.

I shivered. There was a commission on the table—if I

accepted it—and the thought of murder hit too close to home.

"Listen. You have a choice. You can go down the street to Chen, with his handheld needle and bottle of India ink. It'll cost you twice as much and take all day. Dip and stab. Prick by maddening prick." I paused to make sure I had his attention. I did. "Or you can roll up your sleeve and my 'contraption' will get it done in a fraction of the time. Hurts less too." I made that last part up. He believed it though.

It's all about the sell.

Viktor shrugged out of his wrinkled waistcoat and plunked two silver pieces on the table. I scooped them up. It wouldn't cover rent. I was going to have to take the commission. I promised myself it was the last time.

Cross my heart.

I omitted the 'hope to die' part, refusing to think about it.

I sized Viktor up. He'd require a bit more than the last guy. It took some quick mental athletics to calculate the proper dosage. I turned the black knob a quarter turn.

Bless the Queen, he's massive.

I nudged the dial a little more to compensate. Just a hair.

With a flip of a switch the machine jolted to life. Steam flowed, the gears jerked forward. Pressure built, and the sprockets caught, turning the cogs more smoothly, and the needle began to buzz. The ink flowed, and I settled in to draw.

I hate sailors. They always want mermaids.

The Marquis was late. I'd almost given up when the steam-cart pulled up to the alley. *Idiot.* It stood out, belching clouds of white and clattering on the cobblestones. As he hopped out, he yanked off his goggles. They dangled around his neck, stark against a paisley ascot. The robin's egg blue fabric captivated me. I'd never be able to keep something that delicate so pristine. I stuffed ink-stained fingers in my pockets.

"Is it done?" The Marquis pitched his voice low. Conspiratorial. His dark eyes twinkled, as if this were all a game.

The blunderbuss in the Marquis's belt caught my eye. I had to do this carefully. "The poison in the ink is slow acting, but it's done." I hedged and hoped it was enough.

He pulled a purse out of his satiny waistcoat and bounced it on his hand. Coins jingled, loud in the hush of the alley. He grinned. Cruel, not mirthful. "Excellent. For years he's—"

I held my hand up to interrupt. "Save it. I don't want to know. I've done what you've asked. Viktor won't be on the boat tomorrow." I hated listening to the confessionals. I just wanted out of there before the Marquis found out the truth. The poison wouldn't kill Viktor, but it would make him too ill to sail. That's what I was being paid for. Technically. To keep him from making the boat.

The purse landed with a thunk at my feet. I snatched it up and melted into the shadows without a word.

The lighter worked down the street, lamppost to lamppost. I watched as he twisted a knob to get the gas flowing. He reached up with a pole, pulled a lever, and the tip of the device sparked. A warm glow spilled through the glass as he moved on to the next gaslight.

Delightful.

Strolling through the upscale marketplace, I pretended

I belonged. As if I could afford the luxuries for sale in the windows of the boutiques. In the growing shadows of evening, I could ignore my threadbare coat and scuffed boots. The weight of silver against my hip was both comfort and temptation. It fueled the desire to take another commission.

No, Augustus. You want to get yourself killed? That was the last one.

Evening deepened and lights from the boutiques winked on. I lingered in front of a hatter's shop. A silk stovepipe perched on a stand, jaunty in the display window. I fingered my purse, wistful. It was spent coin—rent and ink would devour it. Not to mention the coal for the steam. I sighed. Lord, I'd look rakish in that hat. I couldn't afford it though. Not if I wanted to eat.

I turned back down the street. The clack of heels on cobbles followed me. I lengthened my stride, but the footsteps kept pace. A thrill of fear raised the hairs on the back of my neck. I tried to be nonchalant, glancing over my shoulder. Shadows danced, the gaslights suddenly dim behind bug splattered glass. The flickering flames seemed unable to dispel the darkness.

It was too soon for the Marquis to realize that Viktor wasn't dead. Who then? Some other client looking to tie up loose ends? A thief?

No, there aren't footpads in this part of the city.

I turned the corner and the unseen stranger followed.

Bollocks.

I'd always known that my lifestyle would catch up to me, eventually. A cold chill rippled down my back as I imagined a knife slipping between my ribs. I picked up the pace, struggling not to break into a run.

A horn blasted. I skittered to a halt, nearly flattened by a gear-bike. The driver shook his fist at me as he careened down the street, coattails flapping. I gulped air, trying to slow my racing heart.

A delicate, gloved hand slipped in to hook my arm, and I nearly jumped out of my skin.

"You really must be more careful." Her voice was airy; it swished in concert with layered petticoats. A velvet hat with a lace veil hid her eyes. "I'm Alice..." She wasn't —that I knew for sure. "I hear that you might occasionally offer a unique *service?"*

Inwardly, I cringed. I had sworn I was done taking commissions. It was getting too dangerous.

Unbidden, an image of the black top hat swam in my vision.

You'd really look dapper in that hat, sport.

I sketched a bow. "Madam, I'm at your disposal."

Gwen Katz

Seven Cups of Tea

1

his cup of tea is weak and bitter. It's made of boiled roots, and the taste of dirt is still there. Eliza looks dubiously into the wooden cup. She likes sugar in her tea, white sugar especially, two lumps if she's allowed it. But she senses that she will have no sugar at all for a very long time.

The Prime Minister's face hovers in her mind. His face is commanding rather than handsome, light-skinned, sharp-angled, with a clockwork acuity lens fixed over the left eye. His words echo in her ears: "Little girls don't go to war. What will I do with you?"

The whole ride over Eliza was afraid that she *would* be made to go to war, and that she'd be given a uniform too big for her and made to play a drum or, worse, fly with the Wild Swans. Eliza doesn't know how to play a drum and she certainly doesn't know the first thing about flying. So she was much relieved when the mechanical carriage stopped and there was only a tumbledown house in the slums and an old laundress offering her a cup of nasty-tasting tea.

She drinks the tea politely, for her father taught her manners. At length she says in a meek voice, "Please, ma'am, when may I go home and see my brothers?"

The old laundress is counting gold florins into a pouch. It does not occur to Eliza until she is much older to ask where a laundress got gold florins. She says, "This is your home now, dearie. It's best if you forget all about your life before."

But one cannot forget on command, especially not happy memories. With every sip of tea, Eliza's former life burns brighter in her mind. This time yesterday she was sitting with her big picture book, the one her father gave her with the hand-colored engravings of all the cities of the Great Republic, for he said that a child too young for school could still learn about the world. Her brothers were at their lessons in the schoolroom with the mahogany desks and the big mural of the Graces on the wall. She has eleven brothers, all older than her, and every one of them is clever and charming. But her favorite is Tito, the youngest. Tito is seven to her five, and having only one younger sibling to pass his wisdom onto, he takes his job very seriously.

Eliza wonders if she will ever see him again.

She only half understands what happened yesterday afternoon when the door burst open in the middle of their lessons and a squad of gendarmes marched in. Everyone jumped to their feet, and the older boys drew their smallswords and Tito, who was too young to have a sword, put up his fists. For a moment there was a terrible row. Desks and chairs were overturned and papers were scattered everywhere, and a gendarme stepped on Eliza's picture book and tore one of the pages.

But then her father came out of his office with his hands raised and said, "All right, all right, no need to make a fuss. I'll go with you. Only please leave the children alone."

Late that night she sat with her brothers on a hard courtroom bench while her father stood in the dock. The room was packed. The Prime Minister said things like "seditious language" and "stirring up malcontents." Her father responded with a speech which made a lot of people applaud, but had no effect on the judge.

She wasn't awake at dawn. But when she did wake up, her nurse told her that her father would not be coming back.

She knew she was supposed to cry, but she didn't. Now, as she finishes the bitter tea, she still has not cried. She doesn't feel anything. She is like the wooden cup in her hands, empty except for dregs.

She wants her brothers. She doesn't know what happened to them after the trial. She doesn't know where they are, or even where she is.

She lets the old laundress put her to bed. As she falls asleep, the Prime Minister's words circle round and round in her head, a riddle waiting to be unlocked.

This cup of tea is rich and hot. She spiked it with a generous splash of gin, hoping it would loosen the staff officer's tongue. She's learned a thing or two in the ten years since she drank that weak draught of boiled roots. But the gin seems to be working on her instead.

"So I started thinking. Why would you say who *didn't*

go to war? Well, obviously, because someone else *did* go to war. Or, perhaps, they got *sent* to war. Anyway, that's how I see it."

Through her half-addled brain—for this is not the evening's first cup of tea—Eliza belatedly realizes that she's on dangerous ground. She was careful up to this point. She used an assumed name and told everyone she was looking for her childhood friend who had run away and enlisted. After a decade with the old laundress, she's thin and wiry, her curly hair cut short and sensible. She has the same light brown skin and the same Cupid's bow mouth, but anyone would be hard-pressed to recognize the pampered daughter of the long-deposed Lord Speaker.

But she's not accustomed to gin, and now she's a stray word away from blowing the whole thing. Mentally she backtracks, trying to work out if she's already said too much.

Cannon fire rattles the windows. They both look up.

"That sounded close," says Eliza.

"It's not an attack," the staff officer assures her. "They don't have the manpower. They just like to remind us that they're out there. All the same you shouldn't be here. It's too dangerous for a civilian."

"But my friend. Please, if you could just look up his name..."

The staff officer takes the leather-bound muster book down from the shelf, flips through it, and runs a finger down the page. "No Cantrells here, I'm afraid. But record-keeping has been spotty since the war with the Fata Morgana began. If your friend wanted to disappear, you'll have a job finding him."

Eliza's last name isn't Cantrell; it is Cano. She knows better than to mention that name. She sneaks a look at the muster book just above the staff officer's finger, hoping to spot a line of eleven familiar names, but there is nothing.

"Are you sure you can't..." she begins, but at that moment a whistle cuts through the air. The staff officer barely has time to say "Get down!" before the bomb strikes.

Eliza dives under a table as a shower of plaster fills the room. When she emerges, blinking and wiping dust from her face, half the room is a pile of debris. Nothing is visible of the staff officer except one foot. Daylight pours in through a gaping hole in the ceiling.

Despite the staff officer's assurances, the Fata Morgana are attacking.

Their crimson airships fill the sky, raining bombs onto the army camp. Gliders with bright red wings soar and swoop among them, their clockwork repeating guns gleaming as they effortlessly dodge fire from the camp below.

The army rallies. The Wild Swans launch from their fortified hangar. They shoot through the air like tiny missiles, their riveted steel wings held close to their bodies, painting trails of black exhaust through the air. One squadron of Wild Swans moves in perfect synchronicity, like a dance. They launch themselves at the gliders at top speed. Indeed they have no choice; their biomechanical implants give them electric shocks if they disobey.

The table shakes every time a bomb goes off. The stench of black powder fills her nose. In front of her, gunfire from a Wild Swan fells a glider. It catches fire and tumbles to the ground like a fallen leaf. A moment later one of the great airships fires a broadside that tears one of the Wild Swans into bright metal shreds.

The airships move in. A shell slams into one of the field office's remaining walls and detonates, sending a cascade of bricks onto the table. One of its legs buckles and it tips, trapping her foot. A jolt of pain shoots through her ankle. In a panic, she shoves the table with her shoulder. It won't budge. The gliders are forming up to strafe the ground forces. Eliza reaches down and fumbles with her bootlaces. They're in a knot. She pulls her penknife out of her pocket, slices through them, and pulls her foot free. It's agony to stand, but she does anyway, and sets off for the nearest building at a hobbling run.

One of the gliders dives towards her. Her blood freezes within her as he brings his gun to bear. She glances around, but she's stranded in the open.

Something hard and heavy blindsides her, knocking her to the ground. A shadow covers her—the spread wings of a Wild Swan. Each steel feather cuts a sharp black silhouette against the sky. The Wild Swan screams a wordless challenge. The glider's gunfire ricochets harmlessly off the metal. As it banks and comes back around, the Wild Swan fires back. A hole rips through the glider's wing and it goes spinning out of control.

The Wild Swan turns to Eliza and lowers itself onto one knee. Biomechanical implants cover its body, armor fused grotesquely to muscle and bone, tubes running into the mouthpiece of the steel mask that prevents it from speaking. She starts to recoil. But something about the way it moves is familiar. She looks up. Two dark brown eyes meet hers. It's been ten years, but she would know those eyes anywhere.

"Tito," she whispers.

The Wild Swan winces as electric shocks snap through its body. It launches itself back into the fray.

Eliza lies in the rubble, her chest heaving, as she tries to make sense of what she has just seen. She looks again at the formation of Wild Swans.

There are eleven of them.

3

This cup of tea is sharp and peppery. It tickles the back of Eliza's throat and makes her tongue go numb. The girl across from her drinks it effortlessly, a big grin on her face. Eliza can't tell whether the tea is a test or whether the girl with the goggles and the wild blonde hair drinks this stuff by choice. Either way she figures she had better finish it.

She manages to drain the tin cup and sets it on the table, which is really just a steel tray that folds down from the wall.

"Hailing a Fata Morgana ship with a white flag. You've got guts; I'll give you that," says the girl with the goggles. Between her tiny frame, her delicate heart-shaped face, and her large eyes, Eliza can't tell if she's a very small adult or a very precocious child. She's not what Eliza expected from the commander of the Fata Morgana.

"I needed to parley with you," says Eliza. "I need help and I find myself with few friends to turn to."

"So you turn to your enemies instead," smirks the girl with the goggles. "An interesting choice."

"Not every citizen of the Great Republic has the same enemies," says Eliza. "And war makes for strange bedfellows."

The girl tilts her head. "And what bedfellow have I fallen in with?"

"I am Eliza Cano, daughter of Aristide Cano."

The girl drops her cup.

She jumps to her feet and takes a step back, her hand shaking. "It's a lie. Everyone knows that the Prime Minister had all the Cano children killed. You must be a spy."

Eliza has no way to prove her identity. She has only the truth. "It's no trick. He wanted us out of the way, yes, but even he wouldn't stoop to murdering children. He paid a woman in a slum out in the provinces to raise me and keep quiet about it. Must have hoped some disease or other would wipe me out, but it turns out I'm made of stronger stuff. As for my brothers, he enlisted them in the Wild Swans. They say that they start boys young in the Wild Swans, that their bodies accept the implants more readily."

"And what, you want me to sue for peace to protect your precious Wild Swans?"

"Don't be daft. I want my brothers back. Everyone knows you've been trying to reverse-engineer the Wild Swans for years, looking for weaknesses. I want to know what you know about them. It's not as if I can waltz into the Wild Swan headquarters and ask for instructions on how to dismantle their soldiers."

The girl with the goggles narrows her eyes, but there's a spark of interest in them. "What's in it for the Fata Morgana?"

"My father believed in democracy and peace," said Eliza. "When the Prime Minister seized power on a platform of total war, my father was the only one who spoke out against him. If my brothers and I reappear, miraculously unharmed, perhaps these ideas will make a comeback. If not, at least you've deprived the Great Republic of a squadron of Wild Swans."

"And if you're a spy?"

"Then all you've given me is the plans to a machine we already own."

The girl with the goggles looks at Eliza for a long moment. Then she says, "Follow me."

At the end of the airship is a small cabin overflowing with books and papers. The girl dives into the mess. She emerges with a long sheet of contact paper, rolled up and tied with a string.

"We designed a machine that could remove the implants from a Wild Swan," she says. "In the end it was no use to us—we'd have to capture a Wild Swan alive, and at that point we might as well just kill him. But for your purposes, it could be very useful indeed. It won't be cheap and you'll need to find some very specialized parts, but that's not my problem."

As Eliza reaches for the blueprint, the girl pulls her hand back.

"I don't need to tell you what will happen if anyone finds out you're doing this," she says.

Eliza takes the blueprint.

4

This cup of tea is rich with honey and spices. It reminds Eliza of the fine things she had when she was still the daughter of the Lord Speaker, and for a brief moment she is taken back to that time. She pushes aside the reverie. She is here in the capital of the Great Republic for one purpose, and it's not to relive her childhood.

She touches the cut on her forehead and winces.

"Let me have a look at that," says the man across from her, reaching out. She starts away from his touch. Luckily, he takes her reaction as a sign of pain rather than revulsion.

"It's not bad," she says.

"You're lucky you didn't get anything worse," says the man with a kindly smile. "Why on earth didn't you look before stepping into the street?"

"I had a lot on my mind," says Eliza.

"Oh?"

The man peers at her. She looks back at him. He only sees a stranger who happened to step in front of his automatic carriage. But his face she knows. The years have taken their toll, but she remembers. Light skin. Sharp angles. A clockwork acuity lens fixed over his left eye.

"What could be on the mind of a pretty girl like you?" asks the Prime Minister.

She touches her mouth with one finger. "Oh, I'm embarrassed to say it, but I consider myself a bit of a scientist. I had this wonderful idea for an invention. But I don't know where I'd ever find a laboratory with all the parts I need."

"A lady scientist!" The prime minister barks out a laugh. At her offended look, he hastens to add, "No, no, I think that's a wonderful diversion for a bright girl such as yourself. In fact, I'd like to help. Being Prime Minister does have its perks, you know. Surely someone in my acquaintance must have a laboratory that would suit your needs."

This is going better than Eliza could have hoped. Picking the Prime Minister as her target was a risky move, but she's adamant that his money should pay for what he did. The problem will be hiding the way bile rises in her throat at the sight of him.

She says, "Oh no, I couldn't possibly…"

He smiles broadly. "Please, let me do this. It's the least I can do after nearly running you over. We should meet again to discuss what you need. Over dinner, perhaps?"

5

This cup of tea is strong and black. Eliza snatches a quick drink and then leaves it to be forgotten amid the blueprints and tools spread out on the workbench.

Eliza's hands are covered in blisters and calluses, her nails black with engine grease. There's a burn on her arm where she was careless around a steam pipe. She works from dawn to dusk, riveting together steel panels and assembling delicate gear mechanisms until her eyes blur. And, in the evenings, she must deal with the Prime Minister's attentions.

He has never tried to touch her. Nor has he asked what she's making; once he furnished her with her lavish laboratory, he seemed to lose all interest in it. He seems content to drink nightcaps with her in his parlor or to host lavish meals where waiters whisk the chrome lids off trays to reveal ornately carved pheasants. It's easy enough to squeal and clap her hands like the artless provincial girl she's supposed to be. But her work is wearing on her, and he's beginning to notice.

No matter. She's almost finished. Next week is the Great Republic's annual military parade. The Wild Swans will be there. It might be her only chance. She has no way to test the machine beforehand to be sure it works. She might have made mistakes or the Fata Morgana commander might have given her false blueprints. But she'll have to take that risk.

6

This cup of tea is scarcely more than a cup of hot water. It's made of dregs that have been boiled many times. A prisoner's drink. A last drink.

Sitting in her concrete cell and contemplating her ration of tea and stale bread, Eliza curses herself for her carelessness. She came so close. She finished the machine. But she left the blueprints out, and they were signed with the name of the designer—a Fata Morgana name. If only the Prime Minister had not dropped in unannounced, flowers in hand, talking about an impromptu holiday. If only he hadn't chosen that particular day to take an interest in her work and start glancing through her papers.

Her trial was held privately while the Prime Minister was at the military parade. At dawn, she will face the same fate as her father. She doesn't care much for her own life. But it pains her to think of her brothers spending the rest of their days imprisoned in those steel machines. They will be back in their hangar by now, refueling after the parade. Their hangar is just across the courtyard from the prison fortress where she's sitting, but it might as well be a thousand miles.

Bread and tea finished, she watches the square of light from the high window creep up the wall and disappear. She considers trying to get a little sleep, but it hardly seems to matter whether she's rested or not when she meets her end.

A rattle at the door rouses her attention. She looks up. Is it her time? It seems too soon, but without a clock, there's no way to tell.

But the door doesn't open. Instead, a voice whispers, "The Fata Morgana send their regards."

A click, then silence.

She eyes the door warily. At last she tries pushing it. Unlocked. She opens it a crack and peers out into the prison corridor. Empty.

She slips off her shoes and silently steps into the corridor in her stocking feet. Her muscles are tense, ready for a guard to come around the corner at any moment. But for once, luck is with her. She encounters no one.

A man sits in the guardhouse by the front gate, his head lolling, one arm draped lazily over the arm of his chair. His back is to Eliza. She creeps closer. An angry red line encircles the guard's neck. She prods him gingerly. Dead.

It's a moonless night. Eliza sticks to the shadows as she creeps around the edge of the courtyard, staying out of sight of the soldiers on the parapets. The Wild Swan headquarters juts into the sky, a relief of a half-man, half-bird adorning its façade. There are guards at the doors, but she finds a small storeroom window with no bars on it. A muscular soldier could never fit through, but one small girl might.

Eliza wriggles her way through and drops onto a lumpy pile of flour sacks and bags of onions. The hallways are freshly whitewashed and bare except for rows of long lead pipes running along the ceiling. She creeps along, finding her way by instinct, and emerges into the hangar.

It's so vast that its ceiling vanishes into shadows. Level upon level of steel catwalks and ladders line the walls, holding row after row of Wild Swans asleep in their refueling pods. Dozens of them. Hundreds of them. They stand upright, supported by the walls of the pods, for the bulk of their wings leaves them unable to lie down comfortably. Behind their masks, their eyes are closed. They look almost peaceful.

The weight of her task settles onto her shoulders. All she can do is work her way down one level after another, hoping she'll be able to spot a familiar face behind the masks.

But what about all these other Wild Swans? Who are they underneath the armor? Had they, too, been forced to enlist, built into death machines against their will?

She forces herself to look away. She's here for her brothers.

She finds them on the third level, all eleven of them in a row. Even in their current state, the sight of them together takes her back to those days when they all did their lessons together in the big schoolroom with the mural of the Graces on the wall.

By now, she knows the structure of a Wild Swan top to bottom. She sets about flipping the toggles and detaching the hoses that hold the first of her brothers in his pod. His eyes open. It's Alexander, the eldest. Wonder fills his eyes as he sees Eliza there before him. He reaches out and touches the side of her face. She puts her hand over his. Beneath the implants, it's warm. For the first time in ten years, tears sting her eyes.

She releases his hand and looks away, busying herself releasing the rest of her brothers. One by one, they come awake, surrounding her in a mute circle. But there's no time for a reunion. She leads them along the catwalk and out of the hangar. They are hurrying along the corridor when she rounds a corner and runs smack into a soldier.

His eyes travel across her and the group behind her. He brandishes his rifle and opens his mouth to call for help. But Alexander steps in front of Eliza and raises his hand, making a gesture she isn't familiar with. Whether the Wild Swans have a silent language of motions, or whether Alexander knows this soldier and this is their own private mode of communication, Eliza can't say. All she knows is that the soldier closes his mouth and steps aside to let them pass.

Having an honor guard of Wild Swans is, it turns out, an excellent way to pass through the city unimpeded. The handful of pedestrians and gendarmes they encounter hastily move out of the way when they see who she's with, though that does nothing to quell her tense nerves.

They climb the flights of stairs to her laboratory. The Wild Swans' steel boots sound like an entire army on the march. Eliza's machine sits there in the dark like a maw.

"Alexander, you go first," she says as she turns on the gaslights.

She helps him with the machine's many connections and closes the door, doubt in her own work suddenly flooding into her. If she made a single mistake, the device could tear her brother apart. She squeezes her eyes shut as she flips the toggle.

The machine rumbles to life. Within it, Alexander cries out. Her heart in her throat, Eliza has to suppress the urge to force open the door and pull him out.

At last the door opens. Out steps her brother, clad in nothing but his own brown flesh, marked all over with scars and welts, but whole. Human.

"Eliza," he says haltingly, his tongue laboring to form words after ten years of silence. "You're alive…and you came for us…"

She throws her arms around him.

As he pulls on a cotton shirt and trousers out of a pile that she has ready, she helps her second brother into the machine. That's when the city's alarm bells begin to ring. At the fortress, the gaslights are going on. Did they find out about her escape, or did someone discover eleven Wild Swans missing? Either way, her time is running out. But she can't speed up the machine. Her second brother emerges, then her third. She's just closing the door on Tito when she hears a pounding on the stairs.

Gendarmes rush into the laboratory, rifles in hand, shouting for Eliza and her brothers to put their hands up. Eliza ignores them and flips the toggle. The gendarmes rush the machine, tearing her away from it. One of them grabs a steel pipe and slams it down on the machine's works in a shower of sparks and steam. Tito screams. The gendarmes break open the door of the machine. Tito comes flopping out, his arm still trapped by the machinery.

"No!" cries Eliza.

The Prime Minister enters the laboratory, the acuity lens on his eye gleaming.

"Eliza Cano," he says. "I thought there was something familiar about you. I see I should have put an end to your family ten years ago. Seize them. They'll all be executed in the morning."

The gendarmes move in, but Alexander steps in front of Eliza and holds up his hands.

"Brothers," he says. "You serve the Great Republic. So do I. My brothers and I fought and bled for it for ten years. But is this what you want the Great Republic to be? The playground of a petty tyrant? We were once a free land, a land where anyone could speak without fear. It's what our father died for. We can be that place again."

The gendarmes hesitate. They look at the Prime Minister.

This cup of tea is a smooth Earl Grey with two lumps of sugar. It's the same sort of tea she used to like when she was a little girl. Now, she thinks, two lumps is too many. Her tastes have changed. But the important thing is that she's drinking it here, surrounded by the ones she loves.

Tito sits on the divan next to her. His senseless arm hangs at his side, bits of steel and wiring fused permanently to his flesh. But he's smiling and laughing along with his brothers, and there's light in his eyes.

When the Great Republic held its first election in ten years, the people overwhelmingly voted for Alexander as the new Lord Speaker. His first act as head of the newly convened Parliament was to negotiate a peace treaty with the Fata Morgana. With no more need for a large army, Tito was put in charge of decommissioning the rest of the Wild Swans and helping them adjust to civilian life. The Prime Minister was arrested. Kidnapping is only the beginning of a very long list of charges that are coming to light.

Eliza's role in the whole affair was quickly forgotten, except by her brothers. But she's too busy to dwell on it. She's turned out to be quite handy with biomechanics. She hopes to use her new skill to cure diseases or craft artificial limbs.

"We could still have him executed," says Alexander. "He's certainly done more than enough to deserve it."

Eliza shakes her head. "That's his game. We'll have him sit through a real trial. A fair trial. I don't think the jury will go easy on him."

She raises her cup and takes another sip.

It really is very good tea.

Tea with Gwen Katz

and

Andrew McCurdy

Andrew: Hi Gwen, I'd like to start by welcoming you the *Curiosities Tea House,* where we spend a few pages interviewing one of the authors from our current collection. Your story was a popular submission among the slush pile readers, so thank you for agreeing to join me. Help yourself to your tea of choice, we have any variety your imagination can conjure.

Gwen: The fact that I'm a voracious tea drinker may have crept into this story ever so subtly. I'll have an Assam.

Andrew: Without giving away too much, can you tell us about your story, "Seven Cups of Tea."

Gwen: It's a retelling of Hans Christian Andersen's "The Wild Swans." I had a book of Andersen's fairy tales as a kid and this one has been in my head for a long time.

Andrew: What were some of your other your favorite stories as a child and what was it about them that made them special?

Gwen: I loved stuff like *Redwall* and *Dealing with Dragons.* I loved dynamic, driven heroes who knew what they wanted and didn't let anyone stop them.

Andrew: Tell us about some of your other writing.

Gwen: My novel *Among the Red Stars* came out in 2017. It's about Russia's famous all-female bomber regiment, the Night Witches. Such a fascinating part of history!

Andrew: I see *Among the Red Stars* online. It looks interesting. I read a lot of fiction based around the Second World War for our last edition of *Curiosities* but I'm not as familiar with the Night Witches as I would like to be. How did you discover that piece of history?

Gwen: I was playing Wings of War with my father-in-law, who's a huge war aviation buff, and we were all picking famous aces to play as, so I asked if there were any female pilots. I was really surprised when he told me there were!

Andrew: Are you working on anything at the moment?

Gwen: Right now I'm writing about anarchist bombers in 1890s Paris. They blew up cafés and assassinated the President of France. They were pretty hardcore.

Andrew: I just split a grin, that kind of story is right up my alley, I'll keep my eye out for it. Do you have a regular writing routine that you follow, like a target number of words per day, or following an outline?

Gwen: Nope—like my protagonists, it's utter anarchy.

Andrew: What role does research and preparation play in your writing?

Gwen: I write a lot of historical fiction, so I always do tons of research. Learning about a historical period and the people who lived within it is a way for me to let my ideas percolate.

Andrew: What do you like best about your own writing and what impression would you like people to get from your work?

Gwen: I think of myself as a very populist writer; I like to write about ordinary people who are caught up in events much bigger than them. (I read a lot of romantics at a formative age.) Democratic ideals are very important in my work, especially my fantasy stories. I hope my readers come away with an understanding that ordinary individuals can have a huge impact on the world, even if they aren't royalty, chosen ones, or magic wielders.

Andrew: How often do you read for pleasure, and

what do you look for when you read the works of other authors?

Gwen: I'm voracious, mainly because, like many authors, I have a lot of friends who are wonderful writers. Often the stories I connect best with are the ones with strong thematic ideas that communicate a thoughtful message.

Andrew: Here is a question that hits close to home for me—what advice would you give a middle schooler who says she wants to be an author?

Gwen: Write, write, write! Don't get hung up on whether it's any good or not. The stories I wrote in middle school laid the foundation for the writing skills I have now.

Andrew: Great advice, and a wonderful chat, thanks for joining us in the *Curiosities Tea House,* it was a pleasure reading your story.

Gwen: Thanks so much for having me! *Curiosities* is such a fun publication and I'm delighted to be a part of it.

Priya Sridhar

The Taste of Storms

Nani's hands were always stained blue and grey. I'd visit her at her flat, and she would show me how wrinkled her hands had become. She was someone who didn't mind having wrinkled hands or wizened strands of hair, though she minded that I was going grey.

"You shouldn't stress," she would chide me when I would visit every Sunday, after handling my own chores. She'd sit me down, and then pluck out the white hairs one by one.

"Nani, if you do that, I'm going to go bald," I protested.

She'd then mutter something in Tamil that I could never understand because my family hadn't taught me Tamil. I could speak French and English perfectly but any native tongue had withered as if a sunflower planted in desert sand.

These days Nani can barely move around her flat without a cane. She broke her hip a few years ago, and even though my mother got her to the best doctors, Nani still wanders around at night with twinges of pain. I remember her before she moved from India, before my parents insisted that she at least stay in the country. They don't ask her to wear the corsets or hoop skirts. Her cotton and silk saris shimmer underneath the British clouds. She looks like the mother goddess Aditi from her old books.

We are worried. The Prime Minister has posted notices about not allowing any more "coolies and job-stealing darkies" into the country. I see them as I walk to the shopping plazas to buy fruit and unmentionables. The papers are glued to the walls and smell of rotting tree leaves. I tried ripping one off; only a corner came off. In the news bundles, they discuss how many people start shouting at those with brown skin.

I am born here so I am safe, as long as I keep my head down. My parents do not draft letters to the papers, since they both work in the county hospital. They had applied for citizenship before the papers had noticed people like us. So they were safe. My grandmother should be safe. But we shook in fear at night, when we all thought we were asleep. I spend many nights in my college dormitory staring at the ceiling, wondering if bobbies will knock on her door demanding papers. I worry they will push her down a flight of stairs and break her hip again. We hear stories whispered in the night.

On a particularly cloudy, dismal day, I took a carriage to the train station, and bought a ticket to the wettest town on this side of the pond. My gloves were damp from the morning mist, and I chewed on my right thumb as the orange-faced lady behind the counter returned my change. I struggled with a heavy suitcase and tried to move quickly. It was an old suitcase, one that had once belonged to my Nani.

"Have a safe trip, love," the orange-faced intoned without any emotion. I may as well have been another insect flying past and not attracting notice. Good.

There were a group of drunks that gathered at the station, who yelled at any Indian person who passed. They asked how my curry tasted. I ignored them, and resisted the temptation to buy a cup of water and chug it at them. Instead I boiled on the inside.

Inside the second-class train cars, there were cushions that smelled of mothballs, and only dry crackers offered. I sat and opened a book that discussed the cultural impact of Jane Austen on architecture. In all honesty I had no interest in Jane Austen or in upper class housing, but it was the only book I had in my purse. Besides which, men didn't bother me when I told them about the adultery in *Mansfield Park.*

On and on the trains rumbled on the tracks. I felt the vibrations through the cheap cushions. My eyes drifted. I bit my lip and forced myself to stay awake.

The train stopped in a damp town called Nimbleshire. I got off, lugging my suitcase. It had scrapes all along the side. The streets had cobblestones

I came to a mountain, one of many in a range. They were mossy-green. I wore rubber boots and a coat for the rain.

The last time that I had been this close to the sky, it had been during monsoon season in India. In India, the monsoons are hot and heavy. We had climbed for miles up a mountaintop, until we started coughing. My lungs had burned, and my dress had been soaked from the morning dew. I hadn't appreciated the trip at the time.

I climbed now, slowly and steadily. My boots gathered mud, and my knees hurt. But I kept digging my boots into the dirt path, crumbling rocks beneath my feet.

A horse grazed high up in the mountains. He was a large specimen, brown as chestnuts and happy to have the company. I nodded to him and kept walking. The horse came to the edge of the fence and stared, perhaps hoping that I had apples. I walked away, and its eyes became doleful. My suitcase felt heavier, the higher up I went.

Down below, the valleys and lakes hung like a watercolor miniature. A bright blue pool gleamed and glistened. Cows walked below, bells echoing upwards. The higher I went, the smaller they became.

My arms were getting numb. Part of me grumbled why I hadn't packed lighter. The other part remembered why I was climbing.

The clouds were just a few miles away. I could taste their cool water droplets and ice crystals.

I opened my suitcase and took out a funnel. The funnel was made of ceramic, baked in a temple all the way back in India. It was hot to the touch, and glazed. I attached it to a glass jar that had several switches in it. The clouds in the distance seemed to clump together, as if they sensed what I was about to do.

"For you, Nani," I whispered. Then I whispered a mantra, over and over again. I will not say it here, because I keep my secrets. But it was what a priest had taught my grandmother, who had taught it to my siblings and me.

A chunk of black cloud broke off, and entered the funnel. It twisted and turned, struggling. I kept repeating the mantra as the rest of the cloud followed, rushing at me.

Clouds do not like jars. They like to drift and make their way across the sky, slowly. But I recited, and ignored how the vapor tried to choke its way down my throat, as if it could drown me this far from water.

Eventually, the whole cloud vanished into the funnel. The jar was full, dark, and heavy; it had the weight of a brewing storm. I closed the valve on the funnel. Ensuring that it was sealed, I unhooked it from the jar. The funnel made a popping sound. The sound made a faint echo downward. The cows didn't notice.

Climbing with the suitcase down was harder than climbing up. The cloud writhed in the jar, as if it were a living creature. To the rain god Indra, it probably was.

Back in my flat, I took the jar. Then I boiled water in a saucepan, and then waited for it to bubble. Then I placed the jar in the pan. The cloud had been writhing the whole way in the train. I could feel its cold coils pressed against the old suitcase.

It boiled only for a few minutes, just enough to weaken its struggling. Then I added sugar syrup to weigh it down, and a splash of berry juice for color. It turned a violent blue.

I wasn't planning to do this more than once. Nani had said that when you take a cloud, you have to honor its maker. There are only so many times you can honor a god that you're not sure exists, or cares about you.

I tasted a handful of my concoction. It was electric, cool, refreshing, and yet jittery. It was similar to the mixed feelings that had swirled in me for the past few weeks. I hoped to spread that feeling.

A tiny amount of the cotton candy went in a smaller

jar, this one cleaned after it had once held jam. I wrapped it in pretty yellow paper, and tucked in my bag. Then I went outside, into the cool rain. My boots were still muddy from the hill.

It was a warm night, with splashes of misty rain from the sky. I slid onto the street with the jar, clenching it tightly. Dim light came from the lampposts. I steadily walked, hoping that no one would notice me. This wasn't the time to die from a chance encounter with a highwayman.

The Hindu temple was in a rented building. I didn't believe in the gods, but I figured it couldn't hurt to make an offering. Indra was the type of god to flood a village if they didn't worship him.

Indra's statue had many offerings: garlands, jewelry, candied fruits, and even coins. He took, tall and regal. I placed the jar by the statue. No one would dare open it.

"Thank you," I murmured to him. "I hope you will help me succeed in the second quest."

The drunks were still by the train station. Their teeth were stained from soot and any ale they could scrounge from the nearby pubs.

I had dressed myself for the part: a stringy yarn wig, clown makeup, a dark blue jester's outfit, and a bright red overcoat. Even my own mother wouldn't recognize me in this.

"Nice to see some clown action, sweetheart!" The tallest one jeered.

"Would you like cotton candy, chaps?" I said, keeping my voice level. "I'm giving away samples today."

"Really?" They looked skeptical.

"Really." I offered them candy on tiny sticks, from my

overcoat pockets. They took it. I moved on with my day.

I scoped out my targets. Ideally they would be immigrants, Indians who had come to this country, and who were worried about their way of life. I visited the slums, as well as the prosperous Little India neighborhood, and offered it to the people who sat by the road, or who worked hard to keep the cobblestones swept. They were happy to accept free candy. Some were in a hurry and accepted none of it. I dared not give any to children, even though they looked disappointed.

"You can have this when you're older," I told them as I handed their parents the blue swirls. When I walked away, I swore I saw the parents were sharing bites with their little ones. Oh well. It wasn't my problem now.

The big problem now was getting to the people who needed this candy. Those would be the activists, who were doing far more work than I could. I studied some leaflets and went to the community center. It was a tiny building that had few lights on the inside. When I strolled in, overcoat and all, a few people meeting at the desk looked up.

"Hello!" I put on a toothy jester's smile. "Would you like some free cotton candy?"

They looked up, suspicious. Some were dressed in white suits and Western dresses; others wore saris.

"What does a court jester want here?" the tallest man asked, with suspicion.

My grin faded. I knew it wouldn't be this easy.

"I'm here to help," I said, taking off my overcoat and rolling up a sleeve. "I'm also Indian. And I made some cotton candy."

They still looked suspicious, but less so. I suppose I couldn't blame them; there were some Indians who were anti-immigrant.

"Come, it's not poison." I took one wrapped stick,

unwrapped it and bit into the fluff. Some cotton candy stuck to my clown makeup; I pulled it off and chewed. My insides tingled.

With less suspicion, their leader came forward and took a stick.

"I take it this is more than giving us a snack?" he said dubiously as he peeled away the wax paper.

"It's a show of my support," I said. "And a way to convey my rage. My grandmother's in danger."

He nodded and kept chewing. Soon the others came forward, and I gave them my last sticks. In the dim city hall, we could feel jitters through the air. It wasn't just from the candy.

That night, the streets rattled. I watched from my grandmother's flat window as people marched, their hair standing on end. My own stomach tingled.

"What is happening outside?" Nani asked.

"Nothing, Nani," I lied. "Would you like some tea?"

As I poured a cup for her, my belly sent shots of electricity down my spine. A laugh caught in my throat.

They were marching tonight, demanding something better. It was the sound of Indra sending his rain on villages that wouldn't worship him. I could feel things were different. The gods were on our side.

Nani went to bed early. I sat by her bedside, until her breathing slowed. Then I got dressed, locked her flat behind me, and went to march.

My rage wouldn't go to waste.

Adam Gaylord

The There-It-Is Store

he bell over the door jingled and Claire hastily tucked her book under the counter. It was one of her favorites and she'd just gotten to the best part. She didn't want a customer to come in and claim it.

An older man, probably twice Claire's age, entered the store. Actually, he really more danced his way in. The man turned this way and that, his eyes trained on the ground, all the while patting his pants, alternating front pockets and then back. Claire suppressed a giggle at the sight of his search dance—as it was fittingly known in the trade. The man gave up the floor and scanned the shelves by the door, muttering to himself while patting his breast pockets. "I swear I just had 'em. I was walking out the door..." He passed over boxes of buttons, jars full of jewelry, several large sacks stuffed with socks, and a pail packed with pocket watches before stopping in front of a particularly large crate nearly overflowing with keys. He gave a low whistle, eyeing the huge box with trepidation.

"Good morning Mr. Crowhurst," Clair interrupted his search.

"Hm? Oh, yes. Hello." Mr. Crowhurst wandered up to the counter, still patting. "I really hope you can help me. Do you happen to know where…" He trailed off, his eyes drifting to the shelves behind her. Claire felt the tingle of the there-it-is magic and the man's patting finally stopped, his face lighting up. "There they are!"

She retrieved the keys to his steam car, third shelf on the right, just like last time, and he passed her a few coins with a "Thank you." Claire eagerly reached for her story as the man made his way out of the shop, now muttering to himself about something else. But as his voice faded away it was the lack of another sound that made her stop. She cocked her head but still there was silence.

Peering around a wire rack stacked with wallets, she found a petite young woman in a ruffled dress frozen in the entryway, her small frame keeping the door from hitting the bell. The girl glanced back and forth, into and out of the shop, as if contemplating leaving a well-worn forest path to enter the foreboding undergrowth.

"Come on in. It's ok," Claire prompted.

She entered the store, her wide eyes taking in the rainbow of kites and kerchiefs draped from the ceiling. She ran a gentle hand over a glass case of spectacles and gloves and shied away from a cabinet of dentures, hair pieces, and false eyes.

She made it to the counter and waited, her face mostly hidden by long curly blonde locks.

"Can I help you?" Claire asked.

"I'm not sure." She hesitated. "I-I think I've lost something."

"What have you lost?"

"I'm not sure. But I know it's gone. I can feel it. Something important." She shuddered slightly, her hands pulling her ruffled skirt tight around her. "If, if something's taken from you, it's like you lost it, right?" She looked up with such pain in her eyes, yet such hope, that Claire's voice caught in her throat. It was a mix of emotions that she recognized from her own troubled youth.

This was the hard part of the job. Adults mostly lost things: material possessions they misplaced or forgot. But children, and young women especially, has so much more to lose, parts of themselves that couldn't be replaced at the corner store.

"Some things that are lost can be found again," she chose her words carefully, "if you look in the right place. And for many things, this happens to be one of those places."

The girl perked up a little.

"But some things, once lost, can never be found."

Her eyes returned to the ground. "How do I know the difference?"

"When the time comes, you'll know."

"But what do I do until then?"

Claire looked around the store that had become her home, smelled the musk of old leather and dust, felt the touch of the there-it-is magic. She hadn't been much older than this girl the first time she'd wandered through the front door, lost and scared. Her old master had shown her the ways of this place. Over the years she'd found many things here: confidence, direction, a sense of self. But lately, rather than wonder it was boredom and monotony that more often found their way into her day. Maybe it was time for her to find a different path, a different place.

"Tell you what," she said, "I've been looking for some help around this place. Why don't you come by a few hours every week? If you like it, then maybe there's a place for you here."

The girl hesitated, her eyes flitting back toward the door.

"Plus, it will let you keep an eye out for whatever it is you lost."

The girl thought for a moment and then nodded, giving a pretty little smile. She promised to come back the next day, bright and early. Claire told her to wear trousers and to be ready to get her hands dirty. And as Raleigh left, for that was the girl's name, Claire found that it was she who had found something that day; something she didn't even know she'd been missing.

And the there-it-is magic tingled.

Jason J. McGuiston

Euphonia

Faber had already doused the mechanics of the device with kerosene when I entered the lab, and it took a tremendous effort to wrest the fire axe from his violent grasp. But after a minor scuffle and several stern words, I managed to calm the poor man, and he reluctantly agreed to a spot of tea in the other room. His grudging retreat, however, did not come before I had the opportunity to examine the latest incarnation of his singular invention.

I was at once struck by the smaller, more precise and intricate workings of the machine. I recalled that one of his earliest models had rested upon a sturdy desk and resembled nothing-so-much as the result of interbreeding an upright piano and a smithy. A huge keyboard, coupled to a large leather bellows operated by a foot pedal were clearly visible through the iron latticework, so as to ensure no deception in giving the front-mounted waxwork face the power of human speech.

By contrast, this latest prototype was miniscule, even more advanced than the version I had recently seen in Barnum's museum. The keys had been replaced by a small collection of buttons, and the large bellows by a pair of reciprocating bladders no bigger than grapefruits. These interlinked devices were all encased in a delicate pinewood frame. The whole conglomeration easily accommodated by a small end table. In a word, it was elegant.

As marvelous as I found the mechanical innovations to be, Faber's attempts at humanizing the waxwork figurehead unsettled me. I could have sworn that the thing wore an expensive wig of real human curls. I noted, too, that stage makeup and not paint, had been delicately applied to the India-rubber face and lips. But those green glass eyes were as cold and soulless as the first model I had beheld years before, and they seemed to follow my withdrawal from the otherwise empty laboratory with a malevolent indifference.

I had not seen Joseph Faber in over a decade, not since the esteemed scholar and director of the U.S. Mint, Robert Patterson, and I had encouraged him to present his Wonderful Talking Machine at the Musical Fund Hall in Philadelphia in the winter of 1845. Though the demonstration was not as successful as had been hoped, and the eccentric German had been devastated, I learned that he and his invention were subsequently recruited by P.T. Barnum and had toured England. Though I thought this a terrible waste of such a miraculous and innovative contraption—huckstering for the peanut and penny crowd—I'll admit I was too busy to give it much thought at the time, what with my responsibilities to the Smithsonian and my own scientific investigations.

But as I sat in the chill and unhappy rented room with

Faber on that grey February day in 1859, I saw that the intervening years had been far more unkind to the little man than I could ever have imagined. His thinning hair was long and unkempt and he wanted for a shave. His hands and face, now wrinkled and splotched, were as stained with machine oil and grease as they had ever been, and I would not have doubted that his threadbare suit was the very one he had worn in Philadelphia a decade and a half before.

"Now, my dear Faber," I said once the first hot dram had shaken him from the worst of his rage. "What seems to be the problem? Surely you aren't going to destroy yet *another* prototype. They don't exactly grow on trees, and, if you'll forgive my saying so, you hardly look able to afford the luxury of another apocalyptic tantrum."

Faber narrowed his yellowed eyes through his chipped spectacles, took another long sip, and grunted. "Problem, Henry? Problem!" His German accent grew thicker as his voice rose in agitation. *"She* is my problem!" He jabbed an accusing finger at the closed laboratory where his device was held. "Just as she has always been! She is so…contrary! She speaks and then she doesn't speak. It is maddening, I tell you, maddening."

I blinked at the poor man, then gave a good-spirited chuckle. "Well of course she speaks when you operate her, and then is silent when you don't. That is how you designed the machine, correct?"

"No!" Faber slammed his teacup onto the table. "You do not understand...She speaks to me when I am alone, just as she always has." His eyes went distant and the rage fell from his face, leaving him rumpled and all but empty. "In the voice of an angel, she tells me secrets and sings the most beautiful songs. And then, when I have an audience, when my foot is on her pedal and my fingers on her keys, she groans and howls like a damned and tormented soul in hell."

I cleared my throat, appreciating his candor in describing his device's shortcomings. The words 'sepulchral' and 'haunting' had oft been used to style the thing's performances. And I had always known Faber was an odd bird, inhumanly single-minded in his devotion to replicating human speech mechanically, and given to isolated bouts of hypochondria. But this strange declaration sounded like the losing battle in a lifelong war against encroaching madness.

"I've an idea, Faber, why don't you come away with me for a visit at my country house for a while. We'll put all thought of machines and inventions from our minds. Take in some fishing and hiking, perhaps? You look like you could use a home-cooked meal or two."

He turned his mad eyes back to me. "You don't understand, Henry! None of you ever did. Not when I destroyed her in Vienna in '41, nor when I did so in New York three years later. Barnum didn't even understand when he swindled me out of that corpse he put in his museum. You'll never understand."

I stared. "Then please explain it to me, old man. I promise I'll do my best to comprehend and to help you if it is within my power to do so." At that point, I believed that promised help would manifest in hospitalization.

He scowled for a long while, then finally shrugged and settled deeper into his chair. I suppose he had already made up his mind about things, deciding that a few more minutes spent telling his impossible story would make no difference in the end. "Very well," he said, casting his eyes to the small coal fire burning in the grate. "You know that I first came upon the idea to create a talking machine while a student in Vienna? I had discovered von Kempeler's

On the Mechanism of Human Speech and was inspired by his deductions."

"Yes, I recall you telling that to Patterson and myself back in Philadelphia."

"What I did not tell you, what I have never told anyone, *mein* friend," Faber said, his yellow teeth showing in a wicked smile, "is that I did not truly begin my construction until returning to my home just outside Freiburg, in the Black Forest. There, sequestered away from the distractions of modern life and the prying eyes of those who would either ridicule or rob me, I set to my task with the single-mindedness which has been the one saving grace of my wretched existence.

"Working long hours so that the days and nights blended into one endless labor, I crafted artificial reproductions of the organs which make human speech possible, and with shaking hands I fashioned them together into my first Euphonia." His brow furrowed in angry aside. "Barnum claimed he gave her that name, but I had always called her thus in private...She has always been *my* Euphonia..."

"Yes, an admirable story of perseverance, my friend. You are to be applauded not only for the industriousness of your youth, but also for your unquenchable search for perfection in the intervening decades."

"But that forest is old," he continued as if not hearing my comments. "Older than any human mind can possibly conceive, and there are things deep in those woods that are older still." His eyes flashed in the firelight as the room grew dark and cold. "Things that have become lonely in their isolation and antiquity. Things that need and even *crave* an intelligence with whom to speak, and a means by which to do so. And, as luck would have it, I gave them both."

I remember licking my lips, my mouth dry in spite of the honey-laced tea. "What are you saying, Faber?"

He did not look at me. "I am saying, Henry, that my Euphonia is not entirely machine. Yes, the mechanical workings that ape human speech are indeed the products of my own invention, refined over the years." Turning to face me, he added, "But the soul that speaks to me is something made by Other Hands than mine." He crossed himself at this. "And I do not know if those hands be from heaven or hell."

The shadow of a sad smile drifted across his weathered features. "In the beginning, it was a joyous thing. I had gotten so used to my solitude that I had forgotten the simple pleasure of companionship." His eyes sparkled as they turned to me. "And she had so many things to tell me. She knew the secrets of those woods from the times before the Romans came, and she could sing me the songs of the people who had lived there centuries before my Teutonic ancestors ever migrated into the region. She had known Wotan when he had been a mere man, a hunter and the leader of fur-clad tribesmen…She sang songs of the Forest Lords, gigantic stags standing taller than elephants, with antlers wider than train cars…She told me stories of the Wild Hunt, and of its charmingly sinister origins…So, so many beautiful and wonderful things…"

His face grew dark and twisted again, his voice harsh and tight. "But of late, the things she tells me, the songs she sings are not beautiful. They are terrible and ugly things, Henry. Damnable and hateful things that would crush a normal man's mind and leave him a shriveled wreck, begging for oblivion. She has begun to tell me of the time before the forest, before the time of men. Before the time when the world was made...

"And my mind, strong as it is, cannot last much

longer against these whispered secrets, sung to me in my sleep by a voice sweeter than honey and soothing as my mother's breath."

"This is nonsense," I said with too much vehemence. I felt an unnatural chill at his words and was embarrassed and angry at my own childish superstitions. "You have simply worked yourself into a nervous disorder, my friend. Now, come away with me at once and we will find you help."

He stood and stepped toward the laboratory door. "There is no help for me, Henry. Not so long as I continue to build these damned things so she can keep singing to me." His hands clenched into fists, relaxed, and clenched again. "And God save me, I can't stop! A part of me wants —no, *needs* to hear these secrets; the secrets no mortal man was ever meant to know. Every time I gain the strength to destroy her, that unholy desire compels me to make her again. And each new body is better than the last."

I stood and grasped his arm. "This is madness, Faber. You need help, and I'm the man to see that you get it."

He shook me off. Though he was a small man, decades spent in tooling machinery and carving wood had hardened his muscles, and now a madness fueled his resolve. "This is the last one, Henry. I swear it! I will not keep giving her new bodies until she has powers other than speech. Can you imagine an abomination like her moving about the people of this world, whispering her damning secrets in their ears? Singing her seductive songs beneath their bedroom windows at night? I'll not be responsible for that, Henry. I won't!"

He surprised me with a herculean shove that sent me sprawling across the room's rough boards. In that instant, he disappeared into the laboratory and the door slammed shut behind him. I leapt to my feet, shouting his name as I ran for the door. It was locked. I rattled the knob and pounded on the frame, imploring the poor genius to see reason.

And then I froze. My voice choked in my throat. My throbbing hand went numb and lifeless. My knees almost buckled. Warm water filled my belly, threatening illness.

From the other side of the portal, I heard a cacophony of horrible sounds before smelling the stench of burning kerosene, feeling the sudden heat against the door, the smoke roiling up from beneath it. I stepped back a moment before I heard the single, thunderous pistol shot and the inevitable mortal thud.

Snatching up my coat and hat, I ran from the house, my skin cold and clammy, my heart shuddering in my ribs, threatening to burst. I ran until I found the first saloon. I am ashamed that I stepped inside and poured myself into a bottle, desperately trying to ignore the shouts of *"Fire!"* and the ensuing chaos of the battling fire brigades. Fanatically trying to ignore what had just happened.

It was not Faber's infectious madness, nor even his sudden suicide that had so unmanned me, leaving me bereft of any courage or Christian character. Amid the clatter and crash of the disturbed German destroying his life's work with the fire ax, and before the whump of the igniting kerosene, I heard something else in that laboratory that will haunt me for the rest of my days on this Earth.

It was a young woman's lovely soft voice, saying, "Please, don't do this. Please, Joseph. Not again..."

SUCTION
AIR
VESSEL

Ian G. Douglas

Mary Shelley and the Saint Pancras Ghoul

The church gate's creak was getting worse. Indeed, it squealed like a tortured animal. Mary would need a word with the reverend. That word being oil. Carrying her unusually heavy hamper, she crossed over onto the hallowed ground. The steeple of Saint Pancras loomed ahead, ancient and mossy, like a forgotten mountain. Tombstones littered the churchyard, some at precarious angles, some flat on their faces, half-hidden in weed. Beyond, the river Fleet streamed down from distant London. Coalsmoke tinged the country air.

But another smell lingered, the merest hint. The stink of putrefaction.

Mary walked around the crumbling walls to a simple oblong stone. She spread a blanket on the damp turf and sat down. For a moment, she gazed at her mother's final resting place with a sad smile.

MARY WOLLSTONECRAFT
GODWIN
Author of
A Vindication
of the rights of Woman
Born 27th April 1759
Died 10th September 1797

Somewhere, a twig snapped.

Mary's spine tingled. Her eyes scanned the maze of slabs. Squares, crosses, obelisks. Any number of hiding places for a man of evil intent. Or something not quite a man…

There! A tuft of brown hair poked above the stones. Mary opened the hamper just a tad, and groped inside. Cold metal found her hand and she gripped hard. Teeth gritted, she readied for an attack.

"Boo!" came a voice and a figure leapt out.

"Percy Shelley!" Mary cried as he rushed towards her, arms waving like an inebriated windmill.

"Oh, Percy," she repeated, letting go of the axe in her basket. He collapsed onto the blanket beside her, guffawing with laughter.

"Your face, my dearest, my sweet mab-kins. It was a picture to behold!" And still he laughed, his chest heaving in spasms of hilarity. He threw his arms around her and kissed her cheek.

"Mercy, Percy," she cried pushing him away. "Not in front of Mother."

His smile fell. "Oh yes, her." He glared at the tombstone with a sullen expression.

"Mary, my angel, your sense of duty to your dear, departed mother is all very admirable and that. But setting up a picnic over her remains, isn't that a trifle too much?"

Mary said nothing, wriggling out from his embrace. Percy went on.

"Every Saturday, you pay your respects. But are you not neglecting the living for the dead? There is a young man, flesh and blood not dust and bones, in mortal need of your comely affections."

He pressed another kiss upon her cheek, this time nearer to her lips. Mary gave an awkward smile and pushed him away.

"It's more than honouring my mother, Percy," she replied. He shot her a blank look. Mary fished inside the hamper and pulled out a dog-eared, thumb-worn, leather-bound journal. The faded title read *'A Bestiary of Shadows and Unseemly Creatures, by Sir Horace Davell.'*

"Oh, pish, not that nonsense again."

"'Tis not nonsense, sweet boy. It is a pioneering body of evidence."

"A compendium of fairy tales," Percy remarked, and began combing his locks with his fingers. Mary blushed.

"It's the culmination of years of discovery. A history of demons, foul and fearsome. With this as my guide, I shall penetrate the darkest nooks and reveal the forgotten truths lurking therein."

Percy threw himself down, with his head on Mary's lap. "Or you could busy yourself with a woman's work. A poet's sensitivity needs tending and care."

A woman's work! What would her mother say?

But Percy was not finished. "It is quite unhealthy, burying your pretty head in all this morbidity. Some days I wonder where these obsessions will take you."

Mary did not reply. Instead, she placed the journal on

the blanket. Once again, her eyes darted from shadow to shadow.

"Mary" Percy began stiffly. "These preoccupations must cease. Last year, it was your obsession with the pugilistic arts. It was most unladylike to take lessons from that African fellow. What was his name?"

"To be precise, he is an American, a freed slave. His name is Tom Molyneaux and he is a champion boxer on both sides of the Atlantic. And a most talented teacher."

"Bully for him. But he, at least, is a man. You, my angel, are a slip of a girl."

"But Percy—"

"My mind is quite made up, my dearest. I am ending this unwholesome nonsense for you."

"But Percy—"

"Am I not your betrothed? Do our hearts not beat as one?"

"But Percy—"

"And, last of all, am I not the man in our engagement? So, it falls unto me to take the decisions. For your own good."

Percy seized the journal and flung it with all his might. It spun high, falling to earth, out of sight, beyond the forest of tombstones. Mary bristled, her cheeks flushing as hot as bathwater. Mother must be spinning beneath their feet! Permitting a mere boy to submit her to such indignities. She drew a deep breath, glanced at his face, a portrait of determination, and let the air out again in a sigh. Percy was five years older than her. An adult. Her family were indebted to his largesse. He was a man, her senior, a creditor, a poet with a burgeoning reputation. In short, he outranked her. Mary's heart collapsed. She had no choice but to concur. And yet she felt diminished.

"Yes, Percy," she said in a very quiet voice. Percy

clicked his tongue in a self-satisfied way. "Least said, soonest mended." He began to clean his nails with a piece of matchwood.

An old oak at the perimeter groaned, weighed down with its own branches. The breeze was picking up.

"My senses are famished," Percy remarked. "Versifying is such hard labour." He reached for the hamper.

"There are no sandwiches in there," Mary said, pushing his hand away. He pouted.

"The villagers tell tales of the Saint Pancras ghoul," she said. "A pale creature that haunts this graveyard."

"No doubt to scare their ill-bred children into obedience," Percy replied, sulking.

"Indeed," Mary conceded. "To keep them from this very graveyard. Did you also know that every ten years a child vanishes in these whereabouts?"

"Urchins and ragamuffins vanish every day, Mary. But not by the hand of the supernatural. Seek them in the flash houses on London's backstreets."

The unpleasant odour of death had grown a little more noticeable. Mary surveyed the graveyard. The moss-eaten tombs, the wind whistling in from the river, the sunshine. The scene appeared quite bucolic, and yet goose-bumps danced on her shoulders. She has the strangest inclination they were being watched.

"Mab-kins, your ravings are infectious. Either that or I'm catching a chill," Percy said, buttoning up his shirt.

Mary recalled Davell's warnings. "The Bestiary tells us the ghoul is a vile creature of the night. They originate from Arabia but were expelled by Suleiman the Magnificent. In the centuries since, they have crept across Europe, seeking churchyards, charnel houses, battlefields, anywhere with a supply of dead human flesh."

"Then that's the flaw in your argument, my sweetest.

Not a moment ago, you implied these monsters digested living infants."

"Aha!" Mary cried, summoning from memory a paragraph of the handwritten text. "Nevertheless," she began, the text before her eyes. "Even these abominations must on occasions supplement their diet of rotten flesh with that of the living. The spark of vitality is needed to kindle their own fetid grasp on this world."

Mary listened to the moaning wind, her minds-eye conjuring up all manner of air spirits, latter-day Ariels, straight from Shakespeare's imagination, by way of hers. And then the wind dropped. A stillness crept across the churchyard. As if the very stones were fearful of some coming evil.

"Have you noticed how silent this place is, Percy?" she asked in a whisper.

"A welcome cessation after London's bustle and crowds."

The ancient branches of the oak spread out over a dozen or so tombstones. Sunlight dappled the shade, making it harder to discern their details. Had she not seen a dark shape flit between slabs?

"Stay here," she said, leaping to her feet.

"With pleasure," Percy snapped. He fished a small, moleskin notebook and a stubby pencil from his pocket. "The summer splendour is quite inspiring," he remarked, more to himself. "I shall compose something utterly brilliant. Let me see...I picnicked lonely as a cloud...no, no, think Percy..."

Mary slowly stepped towards the tree. Nothing stirred amid the patchwork of old granite. Yet the sunlight was dazzling. Could she be mistaken? She drew level with the first tombstone. A forgotten memorial for some long dead peasant. Shielding her eyes, she could see no indication of the netherworld. No lurking monsters.

Percy squealed.

"Do be quiet, Percy" she said, without turning.

No answer. Perhaps he was finally learning that a still tongue made a wise head. She took a few more paces. No, each gravestone was innocent. She flushed a little.

"Percy, my love, perhaps you are right."

She glanced over to their picnic spot.

Where was he? Where was England's greatest living poet?

Mary sprinted back. The blanket was ruffled. But there was no sign whatsoever of Percy or her hamper of weaponries. Gone! Mary wrinkled her nose. And such a foul odour. Horse excrement was as sweet as rosewater in comparison.

She darted around the church grounds. No, no, no! The fiend had tricked her! Lured her away, then stolen her beloved and her means of defence, only to vanish without trace. Poor Percy! An image of some hellish entity, sinking its fangs into her pretty boy's cheekbone, tormented her. Tears welled up. This was all her fault.

Falling to pieces would not help.

Mary clenched her fists. "This will not pass." She took deep, measured breaths. The river air filled her lungs and her heartbeat slowed.

The journal! It was her only source of advice. Desperately, she scouted among the burial plots. Ah! There! A few feet away. Mary seized it and thumbed through the mouldy pages.

'While ghouls are known to sleep in coffins or mortuaries, cradling the dead in their unholy embrace, they will seek out somewhere for a den or a lair. Somewhere to hide from the eyes of man. Invariably, it will be some hidden nook or cranny, where they cannot be easily found. Sunlight pains their eyes so they seek out subterranean locations, such as sewers, caves or catacombs.

These they decorate with the bones of the dead and excessive amounts of their bile, which is acidic and a strong irritant. DO NOT ALLOW IT UPON YOUR EYES. Despite the blindness being a paltry few seconds, it gives the ghoul the advantage. And it will not hesitate in breaking your neck with its scaly hands. The creature has but one weakness. Its skeletal nose, lacking human cartilage, makes an easy target. A blow to the nose with a blunt instrument can crack the front of the skull which, with the Good Lord's providence, proves quite deadly.'

The entry ended there. Mary pulled at her hair, lost in frantic contemplation. These meadows of Albion's finest loam could surely not conceal any caves. It simply wasn't the terrain for it.

She stared at the crumbling walls of Saint Pancras.

By the very heavens! Her father had carried out his own researches after the internment of his dearly, departed wife. His casual conversations with Mary now returned, like the light that so dazzled Paul on the road to Damascus. There was a local opinion that the church was old, considerably old. And that before that, Norman and Saxon churches stood on the same turf. Supposing one of those had included a crypt? An antiquated chamber below ground, now lost and buried. The perfect home for a ghoul. But how to find it?

The huge church door swung open to reveal a land of darkness. Deciding it was better not to announce her presence, Mary tiptoed in and quietly closed the door. The stained-glass windows were smeared, allowing only the feeblest of light. A dozen or so chairs littered the nave but no pews.

Mary sniffed.

The interior reeked of mould and pigeon droppings. But that malodorous smell was yet stronger. There could be no doubt of the fiend's presence.

Her legs were trembling. Here she was, alone, without any viable means of defence. But she dared not risk running off to find help. Percy might have moments to live.

Think, Mary!

The church was not big enough for a false wall. But what about the floor? Mary studied the flagstones around her and tapped one with her foot. There was no resonance to the tap. No space underneath. She made her way up and down the nave, repeating her actions. Alas, not a single stone proved loose or hollow.

Now Mary turned her attention to the chancel. She paused before the dilapidated altar, her hands pressed together for a moment of silent prayer. The altar was steeped in dust. It was most inconsiderate of the reverend to so neglect the upkeep of the building. Then, a terrible thought struck her. She hadn't seen the reverend for weeks. Months, maybe? The hairs on her neck prickled.

Taking a deep breath, she pressed on.

Thud.

A paving stone rang hollow. And another! Four in total, right before the altar. Mary gripped one, and after some effort, lifted it clear from the ground.

Not for the first time, Mary wished she could wear the simple trousers and shirts of a man. The frills of her skirt were not advantageous to manual labour. Beneath the slab was wood. She raised another slab. A concealed trap door! She quickly removed the last two flagstones, gasping from the weight of the wretched things.

Hands on hips, she stood back and observed her discovery. Clearly the entrance to an underground cellar at the very least. Perhaps it was a priest hole, used during the reformation to hide away the priests of Rome. And then it was abandoned. Centuries of dust and grime had glued the slabs fast, and that indicated that the door had not been used in many a year. Mary reasoned that the ghoul must be using another route in and out of its lair.

The idea of the ghoul gave her a shudder and she glanced around the interior for the umpteenth time. But for the cooing pigeons, she was alone.

The trap door was a rudimentary work. A rectangle, with two big hinges and a ring handle. The ironwork was rusted up. No keyhole, thankfully. But how stiff would it be after all these years? She leaned over, grabbed the handle and tugged with all her might. This, as it transpired, was a mistake. The ring handle came away in her hands. Struggling to save her balance, she toppled back, she toppled forward and—

The trapdoor gave way like matchwood. Mary plunged through its rotten timber in a shower of splinters and was lost.

Darkness. Mary languished in an overwhelming darkness. A meagre light seeped down from the shattered trapdoor. But it was too anaemic to illuminate Mary's new environment. All she could make out were brick walls and a floor of earth. The clammy air stank of rotten bones.

"Thank heaven for Professor Jukes," she muttered. Mary first met Jukes at one of her father's dinner parties, recognised his usefulness at once, and cultivated his acquaintance. An eccentric man of science, but with an ingenious nature.

She fished in her skirt pocket and pulled out a small glass tube containing scrapings of white phosphorus. One of Jukes' more practical ideas. She held it up and waited for her eyes to adjust. The phosphorus' unearthly green glow crept slowly through the gloom, revealing more of this terrible place.

Mary was in a tunnel. Perhaps once a priest hole or an antechamber to a crypt or...Well, Mary could think of many reasons for a subterranean passage. She stood up and knocked her head against the ceiling. Even though she was a woman of small dimensions, a sparrow as her father called her, she was too tall for this malodourous cellar.

Mary carefully pressed deeper into the passage, feeling the damp walls with the palms of her hands. The route sank deeper. The stench of putrescence waxed.

A noise! A faint wailing!

It sounded like a girl in distress. Had the foul creature more than one victim in its lair? She recalled sketches from the Bestiary, of half-men with fangs and claws, strangling their victims. An urge bubbled up in her heart. *Run! Flee!* She steadied her racing heart. Percy must be saved. Civilisation must not be denied the glories of his poetry. And now that he was in grave peril, Mary loved him more than ever. This otherworldly crisis had crystalized her emotions. Percy was her true love, faults and all.

Mary stifled a gasp. The underground corridor opened up onto a cave. It was incredulous. Buried beneath those innocent English pastures was this netherworld, a schism in the sandstone.

The phosphorus lit up an ungodly scene. Bones. Human bones, both mature and juvenile, in piles. And the smell of death was overpowering, an assault upon the olfactory nerves. As though maggots were burrowing into her nostrils. It was all she could do not to vomit.

Mary stepped into the cave, her sense of self-preservation fighting every inch of the way. *Leave! Get out while you can!*

She opened her mouth, about to call out, but thought better of it. The ghoul might be listening. Instead, she stealthily followed the wailing.

There! Almost invisible in the murkiness, lying in a nook. A human figure, trembling with terror. Mary hastened closer, keen to comfort the girl and make good her rescue.

"Oh," Mary said, as she reached the poor damsel. Only it wasn't a damsel at all. It was Percy, gibbering, his pitch raised an octave by his terror. Filthy, traumatised, half mad with fear, he stared at her with wild eyes.

She thought her heart would break. "Percy, my dear Percy," she cried, throwing herself upon him and hugging him tightly. He stank of mud, sweat and corpses.

"Mary, my precious," he rasped in her ear.

"There, there, my love. I'm here. I'll save you."

"But Mary—"

"Be still my love, save your energy."

"He's above you, Mary."

Instinct kicked in. Mary rolled off Percy, and onto her back. The ghoul was crawling across the cavern roof. She saw his green eyes, glistening like dark emeralds. He slithered nearer, his naked body emerging from the dark. It was scaly, the limbs long and prehensile, his mouth a cruel, drooling slit.

Mary was unable to move, paralysed with fear. For all her research, for all the dusty tomes and folktales, nothing had prepared her for this moment. Ghouls existed! It was no parlour game, no exercise of the imagination. She was right all along. And how fervently she wished she was not.

The ghoul was directly overhead. Its jaw dropped and its emaciated lungs swelled.

The bile!

Instinct broke the spell. With a cry, Mary rolled again. Just as the foul creature exhaled, spewing disgusting, rancid bile at her face. Missed!

Mary jumped to her feet. The monster dropped, land-

ing noiselessly on its clawed feet. At her wit's end, Mary cast around the cave of skeletons.There was nothing that could serve as a weapon. Well, hardly nothing. Mary seized a thigh bone from the pile and brandished it. The ghoul cocked its head and made a peculiar squeal. *It was laughing at her!*

"Have at you," she cried, trying to sound brave and waving the bone in the creature's hideous face. The best she could hope for was to scare the fiend away. Sadly, it was not to be. The ghoul's left arm blurred in an arc of movement. It struck and snapped the bone in two.

"This is not at all how I planned meeting the supernatural," Mary muttered, stepping back. The ghoul advanced, arms raised, claws as sharp as razors. Mary could see from its leer it was enjoying their hideous dance. For every pace Mary took backwards, the ghoul moved one forward. And then Mary felt cold stone against her back and knew that she was up against the rock. She was trapped and about to die a horrible death.

Nothing but a measly yard separated them. The creature's rancid breath swamped her own, an unpalatable odour of decaying flesh. The ghoul tensed, about to strike.

What to do, what to do, what to do, she thought in desperation.

The creature lunged forward. *SMACK!* The creature reeled backwards, scaly hands on its nose, screeching like a frightened pig.

Mary stared at her right fist, extended, knuckles clenched. To her disbelief, her body had acted on reflex. She had punched the damn monster on the nose.

"God bless you, Tom Molyneaux," she said. The great boxer's teachings had kicked in exactly when they were needed. The sign of a gifted teacher. If she ever got out of this bedevilled cave, she would send him a thank-you note.

With a crate of beer!

But she wasn't out of the woods, or rather the caves, as yet. The ghoul was mad now and striding towards her, blood dripping from its skull-like nose. And then Davell's words struck Mary like lightning. The nose was the weak spot!

A righteous fire bellowed in Mary's heart. Here was a creature that needed to die. It would be an utterly righteous killing. Her fists would be doing the Lord's work. Mary tightened her fists and lifted them till they were level with her eyes, just as Tom, with his endearing New World accent, had demonstrated. She leapt at the ghoul, which gave such a squeal of shock. Clearly, nobody had ever fought back before. And her fists pummelled the creature's face and nose. They rained vengeance on its vile features. It may have been seconds, or it may have been minutes, she couldn't tell, but at length the ghoul's face made an unpleasant cracking sound. The right cheekbone fell completely away. Green blood spurted everywhere. And the ghoul collapsed, as dead as the bones around it.

"Come, Percy, let's find my hamper and get you out of here."

"Mab-kins, you were splendid," Percy replied, struggling to his feet. "I take back everything I said about it being unladylike for a girl to box." Percy kissed her on the cheek, and in a rush of triumph, she kissed him on the lips.

They collapsed beside her mother's tombstone, wheezing like beached fish. Mary glanced around at the trees and grass, the greenery vivid in the late afternoon sunlight. After the ordeal underground, the graveyard seemed a paradise.

"How did he take you," she asked Percy.

"The fiend jumped me, spitting his venomous emanations. Stronger than the vapours, they were and gave me quite a paroxysm. And then he dragged me down a tunnel, over there." Percy pointed vaguely to the midst of the stones.

Mary nodded. "I imagine he burrowed many crawl-spaces beneath the church, like a mole. In order to come and go without hindrance."

"A particularly disagreeable mole," Percy remarked. Mary noted the ruddiness in his cheeks creeping back. Her beloved had not suffered any long-term damage.

"Well, my good lady," Percy said, puffing out his chest. "I hope this unsavoury affair will be a lesson to you. Burn that accursed journal. Busy yourself with pursuits fitting for a woman of your station and never seek out hell's spawn again."

Mary placed her hand on his forearm, the shirtsleeve grubby with soil and dried ghoul saliva. "Not at all, my dearest. Davell's writings can no longer be dismissed as poppycock. There is a netherworld of abhorrent creatures out there. I will make it my passion to track them down, and if they present a danger, put a stop to it. This day my life has changed its course. I have a mission."

"Are you defying me, my beloved?" Percy asked, incredulous.

"Yes, Percy, I am."

He glared at her, his eyes aglow with anger. But Mary returned his stare with unflinching determination. He sighed and looked away.

"Surely there must be some morsel in your hamper." He lifted up the lid, saw the array of axes, stakes and holy water, and closed it again.

"Mary, my angel. Take me home."

Jordan Taylor

The Mirror Crack'd

1

"What is your substance, whereof are you made,
That millions of strange shadows on you tend?"
— Shakespeare, Sonnet 53

My earliest memories were of speaking with visions, weaving illusions, and feeling the dark rush of ravens' wings as I ran through the mist. Magic then was a path of wonder, a shifting puzzle of colors, like the stained-glass windows in our chapel.

I chafed at practicing the calm control needed to bring these colors into focus, to see the threads of magic running through the world. My governess counseled patience and caution, but many times she found me searching for relics beneath the Tor, or with my fingers dug between the stones in the abbey ruins, trying to call Arthur's knights to me. I saw myself a knight-errant, questing for the Grail, and felt a close bond with my clearest vision—the Grail Maiden.

With time, I came to glimpse the vast woven web of the world and to feel out the intricate connections between threads. As I grew into a real magician, questing for the Grail became serious research.

My papa's first love was King Arthur. He had named me Elaine for the Grail Maiden and the Lady of Shallot. Our small chapel and rectory were built in the shadow of Glastonbury Abbey, the burial place, legend has it, of Arthur and Guinevere.

When my magic manifested he was overjoyed. Even when I could barely walk he involved me in his research, taking me to the Abbey ruins or the peat moors to excavate old coins and iron tools. Later he taught me French and Latin from Malory, poetry from Tennyson, Rossetti, and Morris.

In this insular world I flourished, yet at nineteen I longed for more. At my governess's suggestion, I began searching for a teaching position. Though Papa hoped I would remain in Glastonbury, he looked over the newspaper advertisements with me at breakfast each morning, debating the merits of each position.

"Oh Elaine," he'd tease, munching his toast, "Here is an elderly lady looking for a companion to do ironing and take her to Brighton. 'Quiet and sober girls only,'' and he'd peer over the top of the paper at me, an innocent expression on his face. "Would that be you my darling?"

"Oh yes—quiet, sober, confined, submissive. No. I want to travel, to quest, to publish! Be a Scotland Yard magician and solve crimes!"

I knew such positions were denied to women. But there was no other I could bring myself to accept—until I found the Roswarne advertisement.

"Papa!" I cried, flinging open the door to his study.

"Papa, I have found it!"

Papa looked up from his books, his round eyeglasses perched on the end of his nose, his pen held in the air.

I bent over to catch my breath, waving a newspaper.

"A noble family. Roswarne. Looking for a governess, a tutor in magic. The daughter," I gasped, "My very age. Sudden onset of magical affinity. In Cornwall." I smiled. "Some people, you know, think the Grail is there."

Papa beamed at me, though I thought I saw tears sparkling in his eyes.

"Cornwall—Arthur's seat at Camelot. Oh, Elaine! It is perfect!"

My governess gave me her magic glass as a parting gift. It looked like a magnifying glass but was crafted to reveal the threads of magic to the observer. She bent with a rare smile to help me hook it to my chatelaine.

I left for Cornwall before dawn. In the cold rain and mist, the soaring arches of the Abbey ruins rose like visitors from another realm above the slate roofs and garden of our rectory and chapel. As Papa handed me up into the post carriage, the weight of the magic glass at my waist was comforting, like a small anchor. He waved goodbye, and from the Grail Maiden there was a flash of white in the garden, the scent of lilies mingling with smoke and peat in the early morning air.

Isolated from its village, church, farmlands, and pastures, the Roswarne manor rose from its woods and gardens, a rambling building of grey granite that romantics would have called a castle. From below where seabirds wheeled and cried I heard the sea crashing against the stony cliffs.

Exhausted from two days jostling in the post carriage, I was brought to the 'little' drawing room, nearly as large as our rectory's ground floor. In my plain traveling dress I faced Lord and Lady Roswarne across an elaborately carved teakwood table, they on one velvet couch, myself on another. It was evening, and a fire flickered in the marble hearth. The room was filled with glass-fronted cabinets of leather-bound books, the head of a spotted leopard from India, a jeweled dagger lain casually upon an antique table. Thick Persian carpets covered the floor, and a tall mahogany clock ticked deeply in one corner.

"Miss Grey," Sir Roswarne began. His dark eyes were narrowed; his black hair fell over his forehead. "Magical ability is not rare in the Roswarne family. But control is taught early and strictly." His pale features contorted briefly, as if with painful memories. "The affinity has come late to our daughter, and with quite unexpected force."

Lady Roswarne laid a gentle hand on her husband's arm. She was tall and willowy, her mass of wispy blonde hair secured in a loose bun. She wore a stunning dress of rose silk. "We…this affliction must be cured, if she is to join society."

"Your father is respected as a scholar," Sir Roswarne said, "but before your position is secure and you can be introduced to our daughter, I require a demonstration of your abilities." He glanced at his wife. "Given the circumstances."

I was exhausted, but I knew their situation was without precedent. A male tutor was out of the question, yet to bring in a female magician! I replied only "Of course."

I closed my eyes, breathing slowly, shifting focus. I was soon calm, alone in the world of light, color, and sense that lived just beside our own. I felt pieces of Arthur's history woven into the fabric of the manor, as I'd hoped. But for the moment I set that aside, found the thread I wanted, crooked my finger, and tugged.

I looked to the leopard, and she stepped from the wall, her body appearing with a fluid motion, her spots shimmering, muscles rippling under her skin. Lady Roswarne's eyes widened and her fingers tightened around her husband's arm.

A white form glimmered in a dark corner behind their couch. A slim woman, her feet barely touching the carpet. Golden hair rippled down her straight back. She faded slightly into the patterned wallpaper behind her. Her white gown swirled around her like mist. Bright between her hands was a silver chalice, carved with scenes of the Last Supper. She caught my eye, a secret smile on her lips.

My heart leapt. It was the Grail Maiden.

She winked at me, and the leopard sprang across the room, teeth bared, claws extended, eyes golden in the half-light. The illusion froze in midair over the teakwood table, and I saw the Roswarnes' shocked faces through its ghostly body.

I banished it with a few quick gestures. The cat faded to smoke, leaving only the echo of its snarl.

When I glanced again at the corner, the Grail Maiden was gone.

Sir Roswarne cleared his throat. "We hope our daughter will be taught to banish unwanted apparitions, not make them leap out at people." He rang a small silver bell, and the housekeeper came to the doorway.

"You will start tomorrow morning, in our daughter's schoolroom. Missus Humphries will see you are fed and shown to your room."

The glass eyes of the leopard's head on the wall winked in the firelight as I walked out.

2

"I barter curl for curl upon that mart
And from my poet's forehead to my heart
Receive this lock which outweighs argosies..."
—Elizabeth Barrett Browning,
Sonnets from the Portuguese

The shelves lining the schoolroom overflowed with books. Velvet curtains drawn back from floor-to-ceiling windows revealed the cliffs and the sparkling, shifting blues of the restless Cornish sea. The early sunlight streaming in lit Miss Roswarne's tall figure and heart-shaped face, her dark eyes and curls, the plum-colored silk of her dress. Indistinct figures shimmered in the light around her.

"You're the girl who's to be my companion." Half-heard whispers echoed her words.

"Your governess, Miss Roswarne. Elaine Grey."

"Elaine," she said, "I am half-sick of shadows."

I looked up and smiled. *"The Lady of Shallot."*

Her eyes brightened and she held out her hand, the shadows of a dozen more reaching out with her. "You'll be my companion as well," she insisted. "You must allow me to call you Elaine. And you must call me Morgan!"

She grasped my hand, my fingers passing through the mists of half-seen others.

"Father says you'll teach me to control my magic."

As she moved, so did vague forms—perhaps a medieval warrior, a tall woman in a long gown, a sullen child reaching for her hands. They flickered in and out of existence through the sunlight and shade. My interview with her parents had not prepared me for this. How powerful must her affinity be, to call these forms out of the aether?

"That is why he engaged me, yes." But I didn't even know how she called these clustering shadows to her. How would I teach her to keep them at bay?

"There is nothing here either," I sighed one morning several months into our lessons, closing a thick volume. I rubbed my eyes, which ached from scanning the cramped text. Books covered the desks and tables of the schoolroom and leaned drunkenly on the shelves.

The magical primers assumed the student was not working large magic inadvertently. The heavy volumes of theory and mysticism not even my Pre-Raphaelite education had prepared me to decode. Morgan and I worked our way through them after daily practices to control the mind, learning hand and finger shapes for sorting through ethereal threads and summoning or dismissing spirits and images.

I feared the Roswarnes' disappointment. I'd written to Papa and my governess for advice; they counseled patience and caution, but I did not see help in this.

At night I pored over books in my small third-floor room, searching for clues. When my head began to ache, I wandered the still house, looking for threads that would lead me to Arthur. I knew if I were found, I'd be severely admonished, but the pull of the house's vast magical web was strong.

Roswarne manor was a maze. Long corridors intersected at odd turnings; twisting wooden staircases carved with vines and flowers beckoned. Intricate medieval tapestries heavy with the scent of beeswax hung over the stone walls, and patterned carpets covered the thick oak floors. Vaulted stone and timber ceilings echoed. Curving corners revealed stained glass windows that by day must cast beams of colored light, but night made them dark arches framing glittering stars or grey clouds. Above each thick door was carved the Roswarne coat of arms: a single rose held in a mailed fist.

I avoided the eastern corridors of the second floor, where the family slept, and used the back staircases. But one night I followed a thread whose brightness sang to me of Arthur, and losing myself in its magic, I wandered where I did not belong. The thread led me to a vision—of knights feasting at Camelot while minstrels played. The Grail appeared, a white doe entered the room and spoke, and an ailing knight drank from the Grail and was healed. The doe stepped towards me, out of the vision. So entranced was I, I didn't realize I'd been found until Morgan spoke.

"Is this your magic?" she whispered. She wore a silk wrap over a ruffled white nightgown, a tall candle in her hands casting a crowd of shadows onto the walls.

Certain she would call for her parents, my numb hands dropped the blanket I'd wrapped around myself against the chill.

The doe darted around her, its hooves dancing inches above the carpet.

"How beautiful," Morgan said, wonder on her face.

She reached out. The doe disappeared and before Morgan's astonished eyes stood the Grail Maiden. As the strains of ghostly minstrels faded she vanished.

I caught up my blanket, clutching it around my shoulders. "I'm sorry. I was following a thread—one of King Arthur's feasts, and..."

Morgan looked into my eyes and smiled. "I won't tell Father." She stepped closer, enveloping me in her circle of candlelight. "Are you searching for Arthur?"

"And for the Grail."

"But wouldn't the Grail Maiden know where to find it?"

"She will never speak of it. But…" I took my magic glass from my chatelaine and held it up for her. She gave a swift intake of breath as she glimpsed through it the tangled magic woven through her house. "Something of Arthur is here." I lowered the glass. "Might not the Grail be as well?"

She shivered in her wrap, her eyes darting about as if expecting Arthur to step from the leaping shadows. A draft swept down the corridor, sending the flame of her candle flickering. She reached out. "Come with me. These halls are far too cold."

Morgan's bedroom lay behind a set of heavy doors carved with the Roswarne crest. The room was softly lit by coals glowing in the grate. She set her candle on her writing desk, stacked with volumes of Rossetti and Tennyson. We slipped into her high, curtained bed and sat facing each other, wrapped in quilted blankets.

She leaned forward, eyes bright. "Tell me about Arthur."

I told her a story my papa used to tell, about the Questing Beast. I conjured ravens that swept around the room as I spoke, Morgan's dark eyes following them. As I finished, they flew into the wallpaper and disappeared into the printed boughs and briars.

A haunting "Caw, caw" drifted back to us. The candle flame guttered.

"Wild magic," Morgan breathed with a smile. "Old magic." She leaned closer, a pleading look on her candlelit face. "This is the magic I want, Elaine." She pulled her blanket tighter about her. "Can I join you in your quest? We could be comrades-in-arms, like Arthur's knights!"

"Comrades-in-arms," I repeated, and laughed. "You must still study," I warned her.

Morgan made a sign over her heart, and caught up my hand, her eyes shining. "Oh Elaine, I'm so glad you've come!" She undid the ribbon that held back her long curls. "Let's pledge, as Arthur's knights did."

"I will be faithful in love and loyal in friendship," she quoted, twining one long black lock around our hands, and I repeated the words of the knight's pledge, our laughter echoing through the sleeping house.

3

"So God me help, said Sir Percivale, I saw a damosel, as me thought, all in white, with a vessel in both her hands, and forthwithal I was whole."
— Malory, Le Mort d'Arthur

We spent winter and spring in diligent practice. During our brief time of freedom in the evenings we went questing through the house. Morgan knew many likely places to find Arthur's magic—a kaleidoscope of colored light cast by a stained-glass window, a tower room overlooking the sea, a doorway and lintel from an older building.

The highlight of those months was when Morgan first entered the tapestry of magic.

"Elaine," she cried, "So many threads—it's so beautiful. Like living embroidery!" and I laughed, throwing my arms around her in celebration.

With the arrival of summer, and Morgan's wistful glances outside, I took our lessons onto the cliffs. In the glow of the sunlight we practiced conjuring or went exploring in search of the Grail.

Wherever we felt the breath of magic—a rocky sea cave where the rising tide almost trapped us, or a clear pool of shining water—we called forth the spirits of the place, asking for what they knew of the Grail. Often they'd say it was near, but by the height of summer we had still found nothing.

Nor had we banished Morgan's shadows. I'd thought as she learned to control the magical threads, her shadows would fade. Instead, they grew clearer.

They trailed behind her like crepe streamers when we galloped over the cliffs, salt wind in our faces, to our 'Camelot'—a ruined castle. There, our mares free to graze, we would collapse in the shade of the ancient oak that grew by the tumbled stones.

"The blessed damozel leaned out, from the gold bar of Heaven… She had three lilies in her hand, and the stars in her hair were seven…" Morgan read from a book of Rossetti's poems, her shadows echoing the words. I sat against the oak, Morgan's head in my lap, her hat tossed on the grass. The sunlight played through the oak's branches, sending shadows and lights dancing over us.

"Elaine," Morgan asked, tipping her head back to gaze into my face, "Why did you not marry?"

I laughed hollowly, and with a gesture sent the vision of a fox flying from my fingers. He slid through the grass, stirring it to green eddies until the wind blew him away in a shower of leaves. "That is not the sort of accomplishment praised in drawing rooms," I said, but Morgan did not laugh.

She spoke to the pages of her book. "If I do not learn to control this," she gestured, her shadows scattering wildly, "I will never marry. I will be the last Roswarne," her voice was hard. "Our home will go to a cousin."

Setting Morgan free of her shadows was my responsibility. And I was failing.

I reached into the aether for the comforting presence

of the Grail Maiden. She tip-toed around the oak. Morgan smiled and wove an accompanying illusion: a glimmering waterfall dripping down the tumbled rocks behind us, fragrant flowers appearing where the Grail Maiden stepped.

The Maiden raised her shining chalice to us and then turned and stepped through the waterfall, taking Morgan's garden with her.

I gazed after her. "The way she looks at us, it's as if she has something wonderful to share…*Morgan!"*

She sat upright and turned to stare at me.

"The Grail," I said, filling with joy, "It healed Arthur's knights! It could banish your shadows! Give you peace. And then you could…join society, as your parents wish. You could marry," I ended softly.

"Perhaps…" Morgan said, "We could pull it from the aether! Not an image, not a vision, but the actual Grail!"

My jaw dropped. Pull a corporeal object from the fabric of time? In my reading, magicians had only succeeded in calling up poor, brittle copies. I knew of no one who had sought the Grail this way. Imagine if I, *we,* accomplished it—freeing Morgan of her shadows, succeeding in a quest and a working no one ever had, and perhaps opening the world of academic magic to women. A smile spread over my face.

We decided to make the attempt at our Camelot. We sat under the oak. The scent of the sea washed over us, its gentle roar a calming sound. I guided Morgan through what we'd practiced so often.

I would conjure the image I knew so well for her to work from and she, with more raw power than I, would draw out the actual Grail.

I held the image in my mind as my fingers plucked at

the threads, weaving it out of the air—the gleaming carven cup, the thin stem, the round base. Soon it hung in the air between us, a chalice of swirling mist.

Morgan closed her eyes, her breathing deepening as she sought through the aether for the thread that led back from the conjured Grail to the real object. Her eyelids twitched as in a dream, her long fingers plucking at the air as she searched through the threads. The wind stirred her hair, scattering her shadows around her.

The image of the Grail shivered, and I gasped. Had Morgan found the thread?

I watched, enthralled, as the misty cup began to still and solidify.

Morgan's fingers flew, the fingers of her shadows overlapping her own. The Grail came together like a puzzle, here a gleam of silver, there carvings taking on depth. It trembled as I struggled to hold the image in place.

Morgan's eyebrows drew together. Her shadows swirled around her, almost obscuring her. It was there, whole. But then it crumpled. The silver blackened, the stem twisted, the cup folded in on itself. It hit the ground with a dull thump. Morgan opened her eyes, gasping. Her shadows went still.

A twisted hunk of black metal lay in the grass between us, foul smoke rising into the clear air. There was a malevolent air about it that made us shudder just to pick it up. We buried it on the cliffs, far from the house and our Camelot.

The second Grail crumpled and blackened as the first had. When Morgan reached out to it, the fingers of her shadows reaching with her, it crumbled to black ash.

The third, though not so ruined, was covered with moss, beetles and centipedes spewing forth as it hit the ground.

The fourth was tarnished and cracked, the fifth flaking to pieces...

Others with more caution would have thought to stop, but each result was a little better than the last. Yet there was something still not right about each one—a twist to the stem which hurt the eye, or sinister carvings on the cup. Our buried cache on the cliffs grew.

"I can feel a pull sometimes, when I'm drawing forth the Grail," Morgan whispered one evening. We nestled in twin armchairs in her sitting room, books open in our laps, cups of tea on the low table between us. Morgan was wrapped in a quilted dressing gown against the autumn chill, her face turned towards the crackling fire. "Here." She placed a hand over her heart, a dozen shadow hands trailing it.

I set my book aside and looked at her, realizing with a tremor that she had grown thinner. Her cheekbones were prominent in the firelight, her dark eyes wide. Her shadows had grown stronger as we worked on drawing forth the Grail, their outlines darker, their personalities more prominent. I suddenly feared that if we did not soon succeed, she would become the shadow in the midst of their bodies.

"Sometimes I think it is parts of myself," her voice broke, "that we bury on the cliffs."

There was something in her dark eyes and tense, thin face that frightened me even more than her words. What was happening to her, and to the Grail?

"We should stop—now."

"But we're close," Morgan insisted. "And if we succeed, all of this," she flung her arms wide, her shadows stretching to the corners of the room, "Would stop, I know it would."

I shook my head. "If! But you are at your limits now!"

Her face hardened. "I know I can do it. I will have peace and freedom. Please, Elaine."

"Once more only," I bargained, fearing elsewise she would make secret attempts. "But should we not succeed, for now we will put our quest aside. Promise!"

Morgan bent her head. "I promise."

She meant it, but her words fell like cold stones into my heart, and I shivered.

"Miss Grey," Mrs. Humphries called to me as I passed her room in the upper hall on my way to bed. She stepped from her doorway, wrapped in a dressing gown, her grey hair in a thick braid. There was a small envelope in her hands.

"This came for you in the post. I would have given it to you, but you hardly ever join us downstairs in the evenings..."

I opened Papa's letter sitting on my narrow bed, reading by the light of my single candle. There was the usual news about the weather, the cares of my fathers' parishioners, his research. Then,

"As to your questions about the Grail, as ever I support your Arthurian research. But remember that the quest for the Grail brought about the end of Arthur's era, and I do not believe it ever was a palpable physical object. The clergyman in me envisions the Grail as a symbol, an image of the Holy Spirit that dwells in each of God's own."

I set down my Papa's letter, my heart and mind racing.

If the Grail dwelt in each of us, was Morgan not, in a way, pulling it out of herself? A self filled with combative shadows, powerful enough to twist any magical means of banishing them?

4

"Out flew the web and floated wide;
The mirror crack'd from side to side;
'The curse is come upon me,' cried
The Lady of Shalott."
—Alfred, Lord Tennyson,
"The Lady of Shalott"

Morgan and I went to our clifftop Camelot while the sky was still the grey of early dawn. A mist rose from the cold autumn ground, pulled into tattered streamers by the wind. Morgan was a dark figure cloaked in her heavy riding costume, a cloud of shadows whirling around her.

"We could forego this last time. We can wait. Study more," I pleaded.

Morgan's eyes were like iron.

I hung my head but held out my hand in resignation. *"Companions-in-arms,"* I said, "whatever may come," and the wind snatched my words away.

She gave a brittle smile and grasped my hand. "To freedom and peace." Her fingers were cold.

We stood conjuring, our twined fingers twisting shapes from the whistling wind. The Grail's shining image formed before us. Morgan took a step back, her shadows fanning out into dark wings.

I reached towards those shadows, finding their dark threads. They recoiled at my touch, but I tightened my grip, reining them in. As Morgan's shadows had grown stronger, and their threads had grown clearer, I had grown stronger as well. Now I could find their threads, and hold them at bay, for a short time at least.

I drew them back into a seething cordon around us, leaving us standing with the image of the Grail in a circle free of shadows. Morgan smiled and gulped the fresh air. Then she squared her thin shoulders and began to draw forth the Grail, her fingers flying, her pale lips moving soundlessly. It took shape little by little, shining silver piece by shining silver piece, a stream of carvings swirling around the cup.

Her shadows fought me, their voices clamoring in my head, warring with one another and me until it was difficult to find my own thoughts.

Morgan swayed where she stood, her eyes moving rapidly behind closed lids. Sweat beaded her brow. Behind her, the first pink rays of sunrise crept over the broken stones.

The shadows tugged at me, and I pushed them back, gasping, black spots crowding my vision.

The Grail was nearly whole. But for one wisp of mist it was silver, burning bright in the first light of dawn. The True Grail, as I had seen so often in the Maiden's hands.

Morgan readied her fingers. I held my breath, my heart pounding. Even the shadows ceased their turmoil.

The air trembled. The Grail Maiden strode out of the aether, her white gown swirling around her like the curling mist, her long hair swept out behind her by the wind. There was fear in her eyes. "There was a twisting in the threads. I see why!" She stretched out her hand, fingers closing around the stem of the unfinished Grail, snatching it from Morgan's fingertips. There was a strangled cry from Morgan, but the Maiden simply turned to step back into the aether, taking all we had worked for with her.

"No!" Morgan's voice grated. She threw herself forward, loss and fury on her face. She pulled the shining chalice from the Maiden's hands and backed away, clutching it to her chest. Her skin was pale in the

gathering light, her eyes haunted, her hair tangled and wild. Her fury fed the strength of her shadows, and they surged and broke free. I felt the wind of their passing. They converged on her like a physical blow and swirled thick about her.

"Please," the Grail Maiden pleaded, turning her anguished face towards me. "Give me the cup and allow me to depart."

"No," I said, "Let her drink and be healed."

"She will not be healed. Look."

Frozen with shock and doubt, I peered at the Grail through the roiling cloud of shadows. The unfinished edge of the Grail was solidifying, turning black. A crack spread through the corrupted piece, stopped only when it ran into the shining silver.

"Would that I had noticed these attempts sooner," the Maiden said. "My piece of the tapestry is in tatters. Elaine, what have you done?"

I heard liquid pouring into the cup. It cast a pink light on Morgan's face. She looked at me and raised the chalice to her lips. She had not noticed the single shadow piece. "To freedom. To peace." She closed her eyes and began to tip back her head.

I ran to her. "Morgan," I screamed, "Stop!"

She drank. The sun rose behind her, a fiery halo around her dark curls. In the bloody light her body seemed to fracture into a dozen overlapping images: defiant, in men's clothes, her curls pinned under her hat, gulping from one of the blackened Grails we'd buried on the cliffs; haughty, in a mourning gown, the shadows of centipedes and beetles pouring from her Grail; smiling, dressed for her first ball, with my magic glass on a ribbon around her neck like a love token; wrapped in a winding sheet, skeletal hands curling around her white fingers; dressed as a bride, her long veil streaming in the wind.

And at their center, a fragile figure in a dark velvet dress and cloak, her eyes closed, drank from a shining chalice, and from the shadow of the blackened Grail, and from the moss-covered one, and from the twisted Grail held in the bride's hands. The sun shone through her, and all the others, turning her to nothing but shadows, to mist.

She lowered the Grail, and the images converged, layer over layer like the pages of a closing book, until she stood whole again. Purple liquid stained her lips. Her eyes flew wide and she choked in horror, dropping the Grail. The Maiden caught it before it could touch the ground.

Morgan stumbled back, her hands trembling as she clutched her heart. "I don't feel anything," she gasped, "but shadows," and her shadows echoed her.

I pressed my hands to my mouth in horror.

She whirled on me, and countless others whirled with her. "Where is my peace, my freedom?"

There was a sharp turning in the world about us. From far away a resonant voice rumbled through the misty air. "Where are you, Elaine? The door is open."

I froze. I had never heard that voice, and yet I knew it, even as I knew my own soul.

The Maiden had gone still, her eyes far away. I raised my magic glass with trembling hands.

There was a tattered door in the tapestry of magic, and through it would be everything I had dreamed of and yearned for. I could feel a warm wind carrying the scent of summer wildflowers, of stone, of home. My heart longed to follow. But I thought of Morgan and stood frozen.

"The King calls me," the Maiden said in hushed tones. Her gown flashed in the sunlight of another world as she slipped away into it, holding the cup.

The doorway closed, the threads reknitting. Nothing

left but the flash of the Grail Maiden's flying feet, the echo of *his* voice, and the taste of wild nectar on my tongue.

I lowered my magic glass, blinking away tears in the rising sun of my own world, and turned to see Morgan bent over, coughing up blood into the brilliant green grass.

5

"...thy curl, it is so black!
Thus, with a fillet of smooth-kissing breath,
I tie the shadows safe from gliding back,
And lay the gift where nothing hindereth;
Here on my heart, as on thy brow, to lack
No natural heat till mine grows cold in death."
— Elizabeth Barrett Browning,
Sonnets from the Portuguese

For two weeks Morgan stubbornly insisted on hiding her illness, coughing blood into her lace handkerchief. I was so consumed by guilt I could hardly eat or sleep. In the end, against her wishes I brought my concerns to Lord Roswarne, and he immediately sent for the physician.

I held Morgan's hand through the examination, her fingers limp and cold in my own. Her shadows swirled in a dark cloud above our heads, their half-heard echoes bouncing off the stone walls.

It was consumption.

Though the doctor wondered at its quick progression, I remembered the twisted Grails, the stain of dark purple liquid on her lips.

I refused to leave her side, and the doctor agreed to recommend we enter quarantine together. An experienced nurse was engaged, her starched apron crackling as she changed the bed linens or aired the room.

The disease drained Morgan's joy and strength, leaving her little more than a shadow herself. She was no longer strong enough to weave illusions or enter the tapestry of magic, so I gave her my magic glass, helping her hold it up to gaze at the threads or watch as I wove illusions to amuse her. She slept with the glass by her pillow, her white fingers curled around its brass handle.

The nurse watched me closely, but I showed no signs of Morgan's disease. Unable to join in her suffering or take the illness upon myself, I pushed to the edge of exhaustion to battle her shadows, determined she would spend her last moments in peace.

At night, as the nurse slept in a corner of the room and Morgan turned feverishly in her bed, I picked my way through the threads of her shadows, unweaving what webs I could, and disentangling from her some of the weaker ones.

At the last, only the strongest few remained, and those I could now keep well enough away, struggle though they did.

Morgan had been in quarantine for over a month when she called me to her, the nurse having left the room on an errand. Her voice was hoarse and weak. There were dark circles under her eyes, and her cheekbones were sharp under the flush of consumption. She lay against her pillows, her dark hair falling around her.

She reached out to me, twining her fingers in mine, and laughed, a weak sound that shook her thin chest. She drew me close, and I buried my face in her sweet-smelling hair. "Will you forget me," she whispered, "when you are away on adventures?"

I drew back in shock, wiping tears from my cheeks. "Never."

She looked into my eyes. "Then find me." She pressed the magic glass into my hands. "Please, Elaine. Find me."

"I will find you." I cradled her hand. *"Charon or the grim King's dog could not prevent me then from carrying you up into the fields of light."*

"Always reckless...one more reason I love you, Elaine."

A week later, curtains were drawn and clocks were stopped.

Lord Roswarne wandered the house with stooped shoulders, his jacket hanging loosely on his frame. If we happened to pass, he would turn his face, as if the sight of me pained him. Lady Roswarne flitted from room to room in his wake, her lovely eyebrows drawn together, her soft hair falling loose from its pins.

Morgan's remaining shadows attended her burial, watching me from the edge of the gathering, until they too disappeared, scattered into shreds of mist by the cold wind.

Back home, I stood on a dark precipice. I longed to tear through the web, to force open a door to a world where Morgan was happy and whole. To be heedless of the threads I tangled, to scream and pound the floor until the magic yielded her up.

But Papa understood enough of what had happened to fill my time with all that the winter celebrations require. Though I wished to fall into the abyss, I instead went through the motions of carols, cards, and Christmas candles, of decorating the tree, gift making, baking, and visits with parishioners. It left me hollow, but as ghost stories began around the fire on Christmas Eve, the never-heeded advice of patience and caution rose unbidden like a guilty ghost and stayed my wild intentions.

These days I occupy myself in our study. Under the

name Gawain Grey, I advise Scotland Yard and provide women and men with magical instruction by correspondence. Often I find myself counseling patience and caution. Magic, I have learned, is not a road travelled lightly; indeed it is not a road at all but a wild wood. Still, I search for a door, and document my research into the Grail. The wages I received as Morgan's governess I have set aside, and if I am able to earn enough through teaching and the publication of my research, I will travel and study.

I keep my magic glass with me always, a lock of Morgan's dark hair tied around the handle. When the darkness threatens I walk upon the Tor with a conjured stag, cold mist wreathing the world below in shadows. I imagine Morgan, pacing as I pace, searching as I do for a door.

Sometimes I look for her, my fingers dug between the stones in the abbey ruins, or wrapped around the bones in the tarry peat, or twisting shapes from the night wind. Often I feel the Grail Maiden watching, catch the glimmer of her white dress or the sad look on her still face, and then I hear Arthur's voice as I had on the cliffs. I feel the warm wind on my face, smell the scent of wildflowers, taste the nectar on my tongue.

One day I will find Morgan, and Arthur. In the reflection in the stained glass, in the crossing of the tapestry's threads, on the other side of the stars.

Somewhere, there is an open door.

Shaun van Rensburg

The Night Bazaar

It starts as a whisper.

The locals flock to it. They come when the sun has set, the stars in full twinkle, hoping that the rumours are true. Many of them have heard the stories before, of strange things lurking in the books that are bought there, of shrunken heads and charms for sale. Some say you should stay away, but eventually everyone succumbs to the curiosity.

It's a very dark place—not in colour, but in product. The stalls are manned by the strangest of people: fortune tellers sell their tarot decks of enchanted images that come to life underneath the moonlight, sinister clowns smile as they show you their collections of bottled laughter and witchdoctors teach their trade around campfires. A smell lingers in the air, the smell of spices and chocolate, and the sounds of bells and voices fill the world around you.

Amongst the guests and visitors, a woman sits shyly.

Atop her head, a large hat is perched, and she doesn't seem to notice the birds that have made their nests in it. She looks at the people that enter and leave—some going with reluctance, others approaching with hesitation—but she doesn't move. There is a blanket touching the hem of her skirts, it displays a wide collection of pretty trinkets, but none seem interested in what she has to offer. None, except a little boy by the name of Tom Jones.

Little Tom had always had a fondness for clouds. No one ever understood why he sat in the rain to look at the grey sky, nor did they understand why he preferred to sleep amongst the grass and dirt at dusk and dawn, and this made him sad. Little Tom could not explain why he did what he did. It was not that he didn't want to, but because he had never spoken a single word in his life.

Not once. Not ever.

The truth was, he really did want to share his fascination with the world. He thought it would be a jolly bit of fun to show others what a wonderful thing they didn't see. And that is why he had sneaked out of the house on this evening, to come here, to inspect the Night Bazaar. He had heard the whispers, the tales of the "weird" place. He had heard them louder than anyone, because no one noticed him as he observed, and had placed it upon himself to venture out and find his voice.

He had explored the Bazaar before approaching the woman with birds in her hat, he had seen marvellous and terrible things. A man who sold fingers, human fingers that crawled around in their terrariums like worms, had offered him one at a bargain. There had also been a tent filled with little flaming candles of all shapes and sizes, and Tom thought their lights were pretty in an ominous sort of way. The woman who worked there had explained their purpose to him:

"Each one of these represents a love between two people," she had said. "Some will flicker and fade, others will never die."

It was a breathtaking place, but he had not found what he was looking for. Candles wouldn't help him, and fingerworms had no ideal purpose that he knew of.

He had given up on finding something that would present him with the power of speech, it was almost midnight and he was tired. Yet, just as he was about to leave, the woman had caught his eye.

It wasn't her hat or her pretty trinkets. The thing that drew Little Tom to the shy woman was her silence. While all the other salespeople tried to barter with customers, tried to sell them things they didn't want or need, this woman sat and observed the people pass her by like she had nothing to offer them. Tom Jones, however, knew that most quiet people have a great deal that they could offer the world, if they were only given a chance.

Meanwhile, we travel through the Bazaar, amongst the stalls of the strange and questionable, and we find the same woman sitting in front of her trinkets at the opposite end of the dark market. As before, nobody seems to notice her, nobody finds it strange that birds have made nests in her hat —nobody, except another little boy named Jane Thompson.

Now, what one needs to understand about Jane is that he was born a girl. And, just as nobody had understood Little Tom, so did nobody understand Jane. Yes, Jane had a voice, and he had the power to raise it, but nobody listened, nobody cared, nobody ever understood.

Jane had heard the rumours that sprung up around the town as the Night Bazaar had arrived—murmurs filled with magic and fear. His heart had given a little leap when he heard the stories of what supposedly occurred here, in the shadows and amongst the people of the night. For, you see, little Jane had lost hope in the world years ago, at an age much too young to lose hope in anything. He didn't think about it too often, it hurt too much.

Tonight Jane had come to the Bazaar, dressed in his brother's clothes, to try and find hope again. Whether it came in the form of a spell, or in the form of a little escape, he didn't care. He too had wandered through the maze of stalls, navigating them with a cautious interest and had seen things that can never be unseen: crystal balls filled with hazy images, a man selling lockets that smelled of cake, and a woman who fed writhing roses their fill of rats and mice. But, just like Little Tom, Jane's night was about to come to an end, seemingly without the results which he had hoped for.

That's when he also spotted the woman.

On this occasion, Jane wasn't drawn to her because of her silence, and he didn't seem to notice her blanket at all. Jane noticed the birds. He had always liked birds, admired them for their pride in their feathers, no matter how dull or how colourful. They had a strange air of freedom to them that appealed to him in some way. They could spread their wings and fly when trouble struck, they sang their songs no matter what day it was. Seeing birds that chose to stay in a hat was a peculiar and marvellous thing for Jane. It was special in some way.

Both Jane and Tom approached the woman at the same time.

She smiled at Tom, it was soft and warm. She didn't speak, didn't make a sound really. Tom looked at her with a curious gaze, and smiled too. He could tell she was friendly, he could feel it somehow, somewhere in his chest. He looked at her trinkets: lockets and rings and all manner of things. They were pretty, every single one of them. Some were rusted and old, some were gleaming and new, but they were beautiful.

She moved then, retrieving something at the far corner of the blanket. She presented him with a silver locket, small and shiny.

He carefully took it, and opened it, a smile spreading across his face. Inside the locket, a blue sky moved. White, puffy clouds hung in the air and drifted slowly by, ushered gently forward by an unseen wind. It was magnificent. One of the most beautiful pieces of magic he had ever seen, and he wanted to convey this to the woman, to show her his surprise and wonder.

When he looked up, however, she was gone.

On the opposite side of the Bazaar, as Jane stood in front of the woman, he looked at the pretty little birds that twittered in her hat.

"Do you know why they stay?" asked the woman, to Jane's surprise.

He shook his head.

"They stay because they can't fly yet. One day, when they are brave enough to take a leap forward, they will spread their wings and soar."

"But what happens if they fall?" said Jane.

The woman smiled.

"If they fall, I will help them up," she said. "And then they will try again."

"Won't you be lonely when they leave?"

She shook her head, making the birds jump in confusion. "There are always birds in my hat, they come and go." She leaned forward. "But, I always wish them the best when they leave."

The woman retrieved something from her blanket and handed it to Jane. It was a little locket, bronze and shiny. He took it and opened it, revealing a mirror on the inside. It wasn't an ordinary mirror, though. Jane saw himself as he could be, not as he was, and this made his eyes fill. He wanted to look at the woman, to ask her what it was, what it did…

But she had disappeared.

Both Jane and Tom decided to stay at the Bazaar, to try to find the woman and offer to pay for the trinkets. That was the kind of people they were, thoughtful and considerate and good. They each wandered through the stalls, looking at the people and searching for her face, then they bumped into each other.

There was a moment of confusion, followed by smiles.

"Do you like clouds?" Little Tom said, reaching for his locket.

Jane nodded, moving closer, both of them quite unaware that a candle flame had just flickered to life somewhere in the Night Bazaar.

A.J. Brennan is a Washington, D.C. based speculative fiction writer and National Novel Writing Month obsessive. Her work has appeared in *The Arcanist*, *Wizards in Space* and *Translunar Travelers Lounge*. She can be found on Twitter @ajbwrites

Natasha C. Calder is from Ely, UK. She has an M.Phil in Medieval Literature from the University of Cambridge and is a graduate of Clarion West 2018. Her work has previously appeared in *The Stinging Fly*, *Lackington's* and *Burning House Press*.

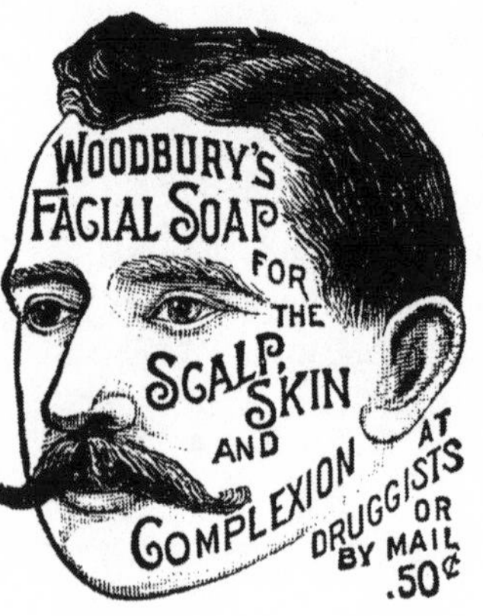

Harris Coverley lives in Manchester, England, where he (mostly) pretends to be busy. He has short fiction published or forthcoming in *Planet Scumm*, *Horror Magazine*, *Eldritch Journal*, and *Shotgun Honey*, amongst others. He is also a Rhysling-nominated poet with verse in *Star*Line*, *Spectral Realms*, *Utopia Science Fiction*, *Jitter*, and elsewhere. If he really had his own "Instant" he would have undoubtedly met his doom years ago.

Martini Discovolante is not a real girl, but she does real work in virtual environments, pixel paradigms, and, rarely now, the tangible world. She lives in a mud and straw box with her heroic husband and two naughty dogs, with a chorus of jackrabbits, ravens, the occasional itinerant llama, and a few elusive humans for neighbors.

Ian C Douglas lives in Robin Hood country in England. He writes science fiction and fantasy and is author of the *Zeke Hailey* YA novels, set on a futuristic Mars. Other credits include apps, graphic fiction, press reviews and the odd radio play. Ian runs creative writing workshops and is a local literacy ambassador.

iandouglas-writer.com

GUARANTEED TO CONTAIN ARSENIC

Adam Gaylord lives with his beautiful wife and kids in Colorado. When not at work as an ecologist, he's usually writing, cooking, drinking craft beer, drawing comics, or some combination thereof. Look him up on GoodReads or find him on Twitter

@AuthorGaylord

JL George lives in Cardiff and writes speculative fiction. Her work has appeared in *Constellary Tales, New Welsh Reader,* and various anthologies, and her novelette *The Word* will be published by New Welsh Rarebyte this year. In her other lives, she's a library monkey and an academic interested in classic weird fiction.

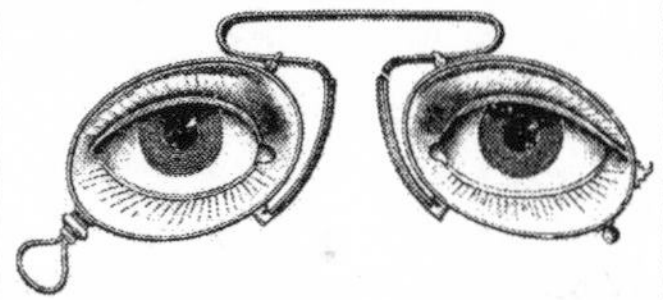

A former diplomat, teacher and web designer, **Philip Brian Hall** has stood for parliament, sung, rowed, ridden in steeplechases and completed a 40-mile cross-country walk in under 12 hours. His short stories have been published in the USA, Canada and the UK. His novels are *The Prophets of Baal* and *The Family Demon.*

Gwen C. Katz is an author, artist, game designer, and retired mad scientist who lives in Pasadena, California with her husband and a revolving door of transient animals. When not writing, she can often be found in her garden or at the local nature center, teaching kids about wildlife.

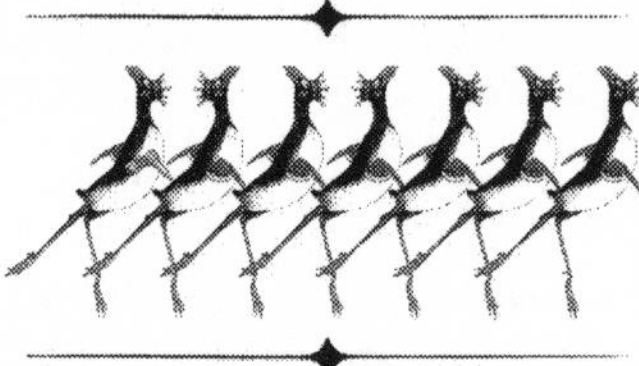

Andrew McCurdy is a writer and editor whose day job as a Speech-Language Pathologist involves helping nonverbal children access technology to maximize their ability to communicate. He lives in rural Nova Scotia with a 12-year-old girl, two ancient cats, and an assortment of feral creatures who have taken up residence in the woodshed.

Jason J. McCuiston lives in South Carolina, USA with his college-professor wife (making him a Doctor's Companion) and their two four-legged children. He can be found on the internet at:

facebook.com/ShadowCrusade

He occasionally tweets about his dogs, his stories, his likes, and his gripes @JasonJMcCuiston

MM Schreier is a classically trained vocalist who took up writing as therapy for a mid-life crisis. Whether contemporary or speculative fiction, favorite stories are rich in sensory details and weird twists. In addition to creative pursuits, Schreier manages a robotics company and tutors maths and science to at-risk youth. Additional publications can be found at:

mmschreier.com/publications/

A 2016 MBA graduate and published author, **Priya Sridhar** has been writing fantasy and science fiction for fifteen years, and counting. One of her stories made the Top Ten Amazon Kindle Download list, and Alban Lake published her works *Carousel* and *Neo-Mecha Mayhem*. Priya lives in Miami, Florida with her family. Visit her blog at

priyajsridhar.com

Jordan Taylor's short fiction has recently appeared in *Beneath Ceaseless Skies*, and is forthcoming from *Uncanny* in 2020. Though she's lived in cities across the US, she's currently a New Yorker with a small apartment full of books. You can follow her online at JordanRTaylor.com, or on Twitter

@JordanRTaylor13

SEE THE EUPHONIA

THE MARVELOUS TALKING-MACHINE.

Shaun van Rensburg is currently studying creative writing at the University of South Africa. He has a strong interest in the fantastic and feels that monsters are usually misunderstood.

for your health, drink

New recipe formulated especially for SHUT-INS cures Melancholy, Time Distortion, Tenkiness, Internet Addiction, and freshens breath!

GRACIOUS COMPLIMENTS
to the Spring 2020 reading crew:
Irene Puntí, Serafina Puchkina, Lori Alden Holuta, Holley Cornetto, Andrew McCurdy, Kevin Frost, and SteadmanKondor

---

Tracy Whiteside is a Chicago area photographer specializing in Conceptual Art. A photographer for over 16 years, she is passionate about turning reality into fantasy. Her work has appeared in over 60 publications in the last year. She wants to awaken your imagination with images of beautiful women in their times of secret turmoil. Tracy's one wish is that she had more time to execute all the ideas that pop into her head because they are bursting to get out and space is limited. You can enjoy her odd mix of images on Instagram @whitesidetracy

tracywhiteside.com

To stay up to date on our reading sessions, podcasts, and print & ebook releases, visit the Curiosities homepage at GalleryCurious.com, *or follow us on Twitter* @GalleryCurious

PEARS'
SOAP
PEARS
PEARS INVENTOR
Produces Soft
AND Beautiful Hands
PEARS'S TRANSPARENT SOAP TABLET
1s
SMALL TABLETS (unscented) 6d. ea.
Sold Everywhere
LARGE TABLETS (scented) 1/- ea.
Delightfully Fragrant.

Don’t
forget
to wear
your goggles